KU-011-787

... AND A
HAPPY
NEW YEAR?

840000426868

Praise for HOLLY BOURNE

"This is a book to press into the hands of
every teenage girl you know."
Fiona Noble, The Bookseller

"Holly Bourne is one of my most favourite authors out there – she writes brutally honest, funny and relatable novels that capture what being a teenager is like."
Izzy Read, age 15, for LoveReading4Kids

"Blazing a feminist trail for UK YA."
Red magazine online

"Holly Bourne is one of the most talented UK YA writers at the moment. Her books are phenomenal."
Lucy the Reader

"Equal parts hilarious and heart-wrenching."
Fable & Table

"Holly Bourne has become a true feminist legend of YA!"
Never Judge a Book by its Cover

"If you ever doubted the intelligence, ability or passion of teenage girls read Holly's books and you never will again."
Muchbooks reader review on
Guardian Children's Books

"Holly Bourne, you're a genius."
Emma Lou Book Blog

"Finally, an author who GETS it."
Emma Blackery, YouTuber

HOLLY BOURNE

THE SPINSTER CLUB

USBORNE

To all my brilliant spinsters

This edition first published in the UK in 2019 by Usborne Publishing Ltd.,
Usborne House, 83-85 Saffron Hill, London EC1N 8RT, England. www.usborne.com

First published in 2016.

Title lettering by inkymole.com

A CIP catalogue record for this book is available from the British Library.

JFMAMJJA OND/19

ISBN 9781474936774 04330/4

Printed in the UK.

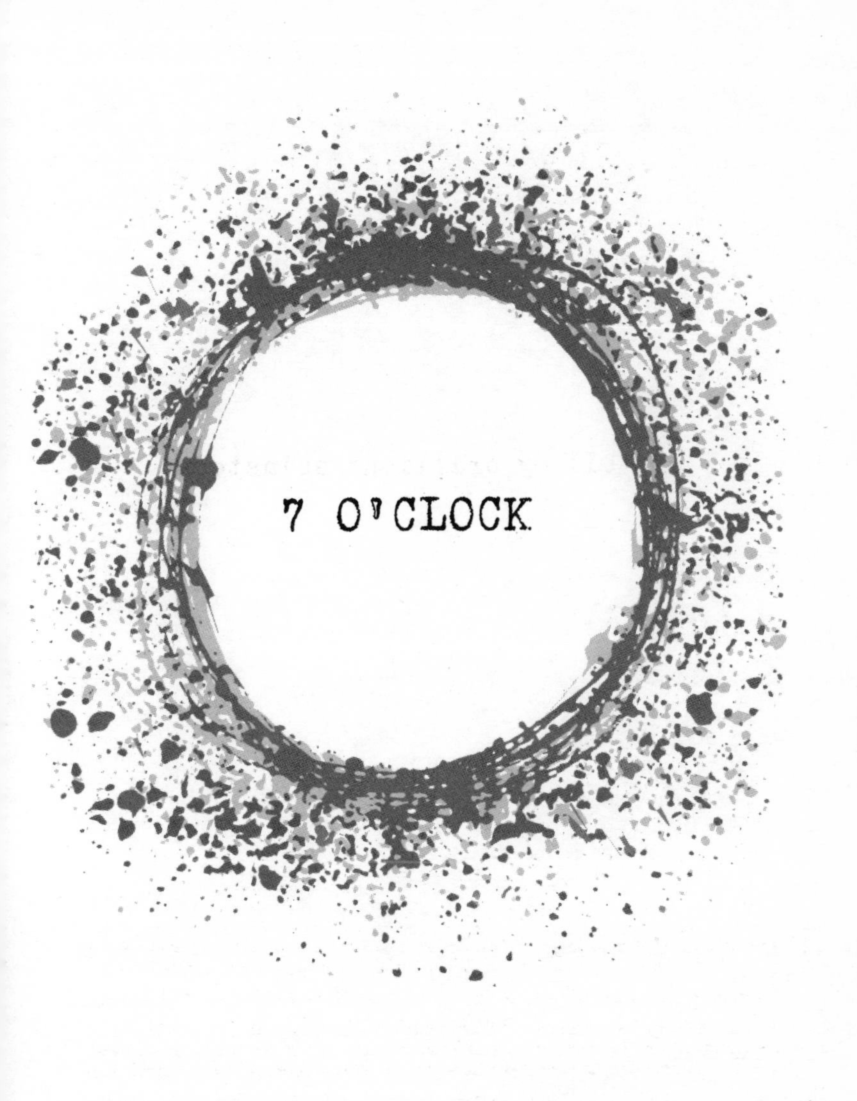

7 O'CLOCK

"I can't believe I'm actually going to have someone to kiss at midnight on New Year's Eve." I took two ornamental vases off the mantlepiece, ready to hide them in the airing cupboard. All breakables were going into lockdown.

Kyle made his *aww baby* face and wrapped his arms around my waist. I had to put the vases down on the carpet.

"You don't understand." I buried myself into his chest. "This just isn't something that happens to me. I'm worried that if we do kiss at midnight, it will cause a giant rip in the space-time continuum or something.

Dinosaurs will come back to life. The grid will go down. Evil Craig will get nice…"

He pulled my face up to look at him, holding it in his hands. "Do you want me to kiss someone else? To be safe?" he asked, in his American twang.

And I thumped him, laughing. "Don't you bloody dare."

"You sound so English right now." He leaned down to kiss me. He. LEANED DOWN. To kiss me. Even after a year and half of dating, I couldn't get over how great that was.

I picked the vases up and carried them into the bathroom; began wrapping them up in towels. For extra protection.

"I don't trust it, Kyle," I called behind me, placing a vase right at the back of the cupboard shelf. "Nice things don't happen on New Year's Eve. That is not what it's about. It's not about new beginnings, or the best night of your life, or your great lost love hunting you down at the countdown to tell you he made a horrible mistake letting you go." I shut the door and walked back into the living room to find Kyle fiddling with the sound system.

"What is it about, then?" he asked scrolling through my party playlist.

"It's about feeling let down by life. It's about a sinking feeling in your stomach that the night should've worked out better. It's about high expectations being dashed. It's about your feet getting really cold watching shit fireworks. It's about worrying everyone is having a better time than you. It's feeling, only ten seconds after midnight, that actually, yes, your problems are still here and you were a deluded idiot for thinking a new year could change that." I threw my hands up in the air. "And, in my case, it was always, ALWAYS not having someone to kiss at midnight."

Kyle held up my phone, which was plugged into the speakers. "Did you show any potential kissers your terrible playlist before midnight?" he asked. "Because that might explain things."

I threw a cushion at him. But, being a jock and all, he ducked and it knocked a lamp off the table. It fell to the floor with a crash.

"Bollocks."

"I think you've found another breakable."

I rushed over to the fallen lamp and gulped in relief to see it intact. I picked it up, cradling it like a baby, and wondered if I could fit it in the airing cupboard. "Honestly, if Dad and Penny find out we had a party, I'll be so dead that they'll resuscitate me after murdering me, just so they can murder me again."

"If you hate New Year so much, why are you even having a party?"

I shrugged. "Because it's New Year's Eve. It's just what you do."

Kyle took the lamp off me to bring me into another hug. I loved how tactile he was – like he knew physical affection was something I'd missed out on most of my life so he wanted to make up for it.

"It will be fun! I'm here, aren't I? And your dad won't find out. It will be fine. We've still got a while before people arrive to hide the rest of the smashables. Plus Lottie and Evie will be here soon to help."

We managed to peel ourselves apart to finish preparing the house. Glass things were hidden. Plastic cups were stacked high on the kitchen table. I let Kyle add three whole songs to the playlist. Bowls of cheesy snacks were artfully arranged. I even put signs up on the bedroom doors, saying *Please don't have sex in here, please*, which Kyle found hilarious.

"But are *we* allowed to have sex in here?" He tried to pull me onto the bed. I looked at the time on my phone. It was seven thirty.

"We've only got half an hour before people start arriving." I leaned into his kisses on my neck, my whole body unravelling under his touch. His smell. His Kyle-ness.

"What I've got planned will most certainly take less than half an hour."

"Way to sell yourself, Kyle."

We laughed and fell backwards onto my bed, Kyle on top of me, raining kisses on my face. His hands creeping up my blue dress, which was too short on me, like every other dress in the universe. I knew the doorbell could go any second. A scrunching sound behind my back – we'd fallen onto some of my art coursework. I sat up, pulling my paintings out from under me and then fell back on the mattress again.

It had been the most amazing two weeks – having Kyle here for Christmas. He'd come for a few days last Christmas too, but stayed in London as Dad still hadn't forgiven him for the whole taking-me-away-on-a-road-trip thing. I'd been terrified about him coming to stay this year. Worried Penny and Craig would tell him horrid stories, that Dad wouldn't approve of how serious things had got. We heard that a lot. "*Don't you think you should slow down? Aren't you both a bit young?*" That and, "*You're doing long distance? Between here and America?*" Like being together for over a year and a half wasn't proof of our seriousness or anything. Everyone at art college thought I was mad.

But then Kyle had turned up on December seventeenth, looking totally weird without his summer tan. He'd crashed college on the last day of term and charmed all my new friends the way he charmed everyone. He'd had Penny eating out of the palm of his hand since the get-go. Even Dad had thawed to him.

Just as things were getting very compromising, my phone went.

"Ignore it," Kyle whispered into my ear. "It can wait."

My phone went again.

And again.

I sighed, and pushed him off. "I have to get it. It might be Dad."

Kyle groaned face down into my pillow, as I got my phone.

Then it was me letting out a groan – of anger.

It was Lottie.

Three totally non-urgent messages.

Home Alone.

It's a Wonderful Life.

EVEN THE MUPPET CHRISTMAS CAROL??????

"Your dad?" Kyle asked, still face down on the bed.

"No, it's Lottie. She's off on one."

"About what now?" It came out a bit more annoyed than he normally sounded when he spoke about Lottie.

Kyle'd been getting defensive recently about how Lottie had been treating Evie and me since she went off to uni in September. By "treating" I mean "borderline ignoring". She hadn't even invited us to come and stay. And her messages were always just vague, or droning on about how great London is.

"She's claiming not one Christmas film passes the Bechdel test."

Kyle sat up, covering his crotch with one of my cushions.

"But Christmas is over already."

"You know what she's like. Once she's latched onto something…"

"She doesn't let go," Kyle finished.

I punched out a reply.

Christmas is over.

Her reply came instantaneously.

But the patriarchy isn't.

When you getting here already? I sent back.

On my way.

I sighed and stood up. Lottie only lived ten minutes away. And though what Kyle and I had planned usually didn't take longer than half an hour, it did take more than ten minutes. Most of the time anyway…

"Come on, we should turn the music on. Get the party vibe going."

Just as I got to my door, Kyle called over.

"When are you going to tell them?"

I stopped, my hand on the door frame. Leaning on it, holding myself up.

"Soon." I didn't turn back.

"The later you leave it, the harder it will be."

My stomach riddled itself with instant knots.

"I know…"

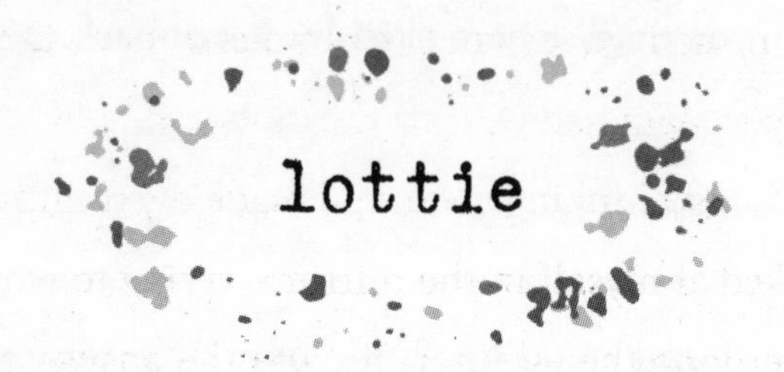

I mean, when you come to think of it, why was it up to the MOTHER in *Home Alone* to go back and check Kevin was okay? The dad in it literally didn't appear to give a shit. YOUR KID IS HOME ALONE, DUDE, AND YOU'RE TELLING EVERYONE TO RELAX? I mean, that isn't just unfair on Kevin's mother, but also, like, the portrayal of fathers too.

God, it's exhausting, realizing things.

I made a note of the film so I could list it in my next newspaper column. I still couldn't freaking believe I already had my own column in UCL's student paper when I'd only been there one term. Everyone at UCL must hate me. But it wasn't MY fault that the Vagilante campaign had made me all famous and that the newspaper team had wanted me on board.

Uni… Just thinking about uni made my tummy hurt.

I looked at myself in the mirror – trying to work out if I'd overdone the eyeliner. *Yes* was the answer to that question. One eye just wouldn't go right and I'd had to keep getting bigger and bigger until my flick was perfect and now I looked like I'd been punched in the face by a panda. Or maybe I looked like a panda because I'd been punched? By an angry eyeliner? But eyeliners don't have arms?

To tell you the truth, I was already a little bit drunk.

It wasn't like I was nervous or anything. I mean, why would I be nervous? It was just a party. With everyone from Before Uni. People I knew, members of the Spinster Club, Evie and Amber, of course – my favourite favourites…even if we hardly spoke any more. But we didn't talk about that, which wasn't like us at all.

I checked my phone for the millionth time that

evening, waiting for a message from Will to say he'd landed. I hadn't seen him since the beginning of December and even then it was just one night. In fact, he always acted like UCL and Royal Holloway – where he was – were miles apart when, literally, we were lucky we were so close. I found it was always me slogging down there rather than him coming up to me. And that one time a few weeks ago when he *had* come to UCL, he'd not been very nice when I'd complained about my housemates. He'd just said, "Well, they seem okay to me," and taken off his glasses and got into bed and fallen asleep WITHOUT HAVING SEX WITH ME FIRST.

Will doesn't do ANYTHING without having sex with me first.

He'd fallen asleep so quickly, snoring, and so I'd just lain next to him in my tiny single bed, watching him snore and worrying about why he'd not had sex with me first. When I'd finally dropped off, I'd got woken up by my housemates coming in from yet another night out they didn't invite me to.

He didn't have sex with me the next morning either.

He'd woken before me, and I'd found him in the kitchen, laughing with Heather, Aimee and Jade. My three basic-bitch housemates, who are so basic and bitchy they make me break all my rules of feminism by buying into that word.

But that was then and this was now and I'd see him tonight FINALLY. His flight from Austria was getting in at seven, so he'd hopefully get to the party by nine. And even though I looked like I'd been punched by a panda, I'd charm him and... What was I talking about? He was my BOYFRIEND, I'd already charmed him! I was just being silly and insecure because uni wasn't quite what I'd thought it would be...and I hadn't told anyone that because I felt too ashamed. I mean, I'd turned down Cambridge in a blaze of glory, chosen a London uni so I could fling myself into a political career and, well, that was impressive even if my housemates really weren't impressed at all.

But I was fine. Will and I were fine. Everything was *fiiiine*, apart from maybe the sell-by date of the brandy I'd stolen from under my parents' sink.

I yelled goodbye and happy New Year to Mum and Dad and ventured out into the freezing freezingness. I messaged Evie and Amber some of my new Christmas-fail Bechdel discoveries. Amber came back to me saying:

Christmas is over.

Was she being sarky? I couldn't tell. I was using the messages in a kind of desperate *look-everything's-the-same-here!* way, to plaster over the cracks I think we were all pretending weren't there. Doing different stuff in different places was changing things, whether we wanted it to or not. And I guess it didn't help that I'd accidentally-on-purpose been "too busy" for them to come to London, so they wouldn't twig how bad things were in my flat. And so "too busy" usually meant I spent weekends alone, staring at the city through my window, or doing "SURPRISE" visits to Will's campus, which he never seemed that excited by. Not even when I brought fancy red underwear.

* * *

The town felt so…small as I walked to Amber's. The streets so much quieter compared to London. It just all felt so…twee and suffocating and like nothing exciting could ever happen or be achieved. I guess if I'm being honest – which I am because of all the out-of-date brandy swilling around inside of me – maybe this was causing the distance between me and the others too. It had only been a term and despite the lonely weekends I felt like the curtains on my world had been flung open. It was hard not to feel like that when my bedroom window looked out onto the BT Tower.

Okay – so my housemates were horrid, and I already had a sort-of reputation at uni for being precocious. But it wasn't all bad. The girls I'd met at the Leading Women Society seemed pretty awesome and undaunted by my feminist column and, well…me. And I'd finally joined a political party! The Women's Equality Party. When I wasn't listening to the girls giggle in the kitchen and feeling too scared to go and join in, I was enjoying myself stuffing envelopes, going around the House of Commons, making posters, meeting all these amazing, powerful, inspiring, incredible women doing fab things.

Our town just didn't have that. I knew Amber and Evie couldn't help it. Amber needed to do a foundation year to get onto an art course and it was cheaper to stay at home to do it. And it was a ruddy beautiful miracle that Evie was doing a degree at all with her OCD. No one could blame her for just wanting to commute to our local university, the one where my dad worked. But they seemed so…the same, and I felt so different, and it was like a huge cheese wedge had been shoved between us and I couldn't eat it all. And, mmmm, cheese. And why hadn't Will messaged me? And…oh, Amber's house is here! I wonder if she has any alcohol?

evie

I lay curled up on Oli's chest, using his collarbones as my pillow. The end of *When Harry Met Sally* played on his computer – the third and final instalment of our New Year's Eve movie binge.

"God, I love this scene," I said, as Billy Crystal did That Speech to Meg Ryan about how when you realize you want to spend the rest of your life with someone you want that life to start right away. "I know it's total Hollywood, but I love this speech."

My head moved up and down with Oli's laughter.

"You're so soppy!"

I sat up and pulled a face. "I'm not! Well, maybe I am. I blame you entirely."

Even after all this time as us, Oli blushed – the red jumping right into his cheekbony cheeks. He dragged me back down onto him and I heard his heartbeat through his chest.

BAD THOUGHT

It's beating very fast.

BAD THOUGHT

Is he okay? Is he okay? Is he okay?

We lay there, watching the credits roll. We'd been through *The Apartment*, a black-and-white indie called *In Search of a Midnight Kiss*, and finished on Meg Ryan. The air in Oli's room felt stale and heavy, the curtains drawn – as they normally were these days – the radiators on too high.

Without thinking, I reached up and gently stroked Oli's face.

He flinched and caught my hand to stop me. "Sorry," he said.

"No, I'm sorry. I forgot." The face thing was only a two-week-old phobia, it hadn't bedded in yet.

I rolled off him, onto the soft carpet, and stood up – wanting the awkward in the air to dissolve. "I'd better start getting ready." I looked around for my bag.

It was my turn to flinch as I heard a loud thump on the bedside table. The echo of it reverberated through the air.

"Fuck."

I spun round. Oli cradled his right fist in his left hand, his face red, tears in his eyes. He'd punched the table again.

"Woah woah woah woah woah." I crouched back down, pulled his hand away. "Stop it, Oli, stop it. It's okay. It's okay."

He looked up at me, his green eyes clouded with water.

"It's not okay, is it though, Evie? It's not okay and it's never going to be okay ever again."

SELFISH THOUGHT

Oh no, not again. You'd only just cheered up.

BAD THOUGHT

He's right!
It's never going to be okay ever again!
What are you going to do?

"Shh, it's fine. Oli, it's fine." I crawled back onto him, kissing his face, being careful not to touch it with my hands. He was stiff at first and then softened into my kisses, managing to lose himself in me for a moment, his hands clutching around my back. We fell into the pillows and, for a while, it was just us. Two people, totally in love, making out when they should be getting ready for a party. I felt proud I was able to distract him from himself. That he wasn't always lost, that there were ways of finding him...even if it did involve him undoing my bra.

Things got hazy. Oli's hands were everywhere – mine were everywhere apart from his face. We giggled as he ran for the lock on his bedroom door. A tiny part of me was in awe about how quickly he could bounce from freak-out to fine and back again – even though I knew my mind was capable of doing the same. Chaos and disaster, tears and panic...and then flipping back to totally normal again. Because you'd let it out. Because someone you loved said the right thing. That's what I loved about us. How we got each other. How there were no questions, no disbelief, no confusion. I totally and utterly understood him, and him me. We were weirdos, but we'd found each other.

BAD THOUGHT

I just wish he hadn't lost himself...

Shh, shut up, Evie.

The thought disrupted proceedings as much as the angry vibrate on my phone. "Ignore it," Oli mumbled into my neck and I tried to. But it went again. And again.

"I'd better get it." I gently pushed him away. "It's just Lottie," I said, reading the messages. Grinning.

Oli leaned up on one elbow, trying to read over my bare shoulder.

"What Christmas film is she failing now?"

Bless Oli, fellow film buff. He legitimately wanted to know.

I read out her messages.

"Really? Even the Muppets?" he asked. "But that's, like, the best Christmas movie ever made."

I kissed him on the forehead. "Which is one of the many reasons why you are my boyfriend."

"She does know Christmas is over though, right?"

My phone went again, with a message from Amber saying just that. I saw the time at the top of my screen. "I really should get ready."

I readjusted my clothing, and pulled my compact mirror from my bag, checking my make-up. I'd applied it before I came over, but some of it had smudged. I pulled out my bright red lipstick, carefully smearing it over my lips, feeling Oli's eyes on me.

"What?" I asked, keeping the mirror deliberately away from him. He was going through this…phase. With reflections. Along with his other phases.

BAD THOUGHT

What if it's not just a "phase" though, Evie?
What if he's always like this?

He smiled and blushed at the same time. "Nothing," he said. "Just…you're pretty."

I felt myself go red. God, how were we still like this?

Blushing and stammering whenever we complimented each other. We'd been going out for a year.

I went back to my lipstick, hoping tonight would go okay. It had been such a strange Christmas break. Amber and I had been so excited to have Lottie back for a month, but she'd returned all...odd. I mean, she'd been a bit off when we videotimed her, but I thought maybe that was just because she was wrapped up in being away. But, since she'd been back, she kept saying stuff like, "I can't believe there's no Pret here!" or "Why do the pubs here close at eleven? In London you can stay out all night."

Most of her sentences started like that now. "In London."

I felt left behind. I felt like a small-town girl, who would never take a midnight train going anywhere – I mean, that is very late to be getting a train! Especially if you don't know where it's even going! Where would you sleep when you arrived? What if you ended up in the worst anywhere possible?

I was sure Lottie didn't mean anything by it. Amber

wasn't so sure. I felt Lottie's constant stream of Bechdel messages was her way of trying...

Oli was already ready for his night, so he just watched me as I put the finishing touches to my face and stuffed things into my bag. His eyes followed me around the room and I felt self-conscious, aware of my movements.

I turned around. "Voila! How do I look?"

Once again, Oli's face had become tearful and tense.

"Don't go," he said. "Please, Evie. Don't leave me tonight."

8 O'CLOCK

Lottie arrived about ten whole minutes before the bulk of the party.

"I bought cheese balls," she announced, flinging her arms around me, a packet of cheese balls slapping me across the back. She smelled a bit of alcohol, which wasn't really like her. Or was it? I wasn't sure who she was these days. Going to London had changed her a lot. She'd even cut her long, black hair into this annoyingly-amazing razored bob that no one but Lottie could pull off. She was wearing skintight jeans and a tight purple crop-top covered in sequins.

We let go of the hug.

"Where's the drink then?" She wandered off into my house, the cheese balls now in my hands.

I heard her find Kyle in the kitchen.

"HAPPY NEW YEAR, KYLE'S ARMS," she yelled.

I smiled, despite myself, and followed her in. Kyle was making that face he always did whenever he was confronted by Lottie. The *stunned-that-you're-saying-this-but-I-quite-like-it* one she often coaxed out of people. Lottie shamelessly flirted with him, but in such a giddy, blatant way it never bothered me. Plus, I was used to girls flirting with Kyle...guys flirting with Kyle...anyone who'd ever met him flirting with Kyle...

Lottie twisted the lid off a bottle of wine and poured it right up to the top of a plastic glass, taking a deep sip.

"So, I've been thinking about it," she said, not really taking a breath. "And there's not actually a huge amount of inherent sexism caught up in New Year's Eve. It may now therefore be my favourite holiday. I mean, Christmas is just a clusterfuck of women having to do all the cooking, Valentine's Day is full of boys proposing to girls in cheesy obvious places, like no one has ever considered the fact girls could propose to boys, or MAYBE WE DON'T HAVE TO GET MARRIED AT ALL. Easter, well, there's not a lot of girlfolk in the Easter story, is there? Just that random prostitute that never got much airtime..." She went on, drinking more, listing all the other holidays. The exhausting feminism tornado that is Lottie Thomas.

Kyle stood behind me, his arms around my waist, listening with his chin resting on the top of my head. "Is Will coming?" he asked, when she paused to down more wine. His chin dug into my head as he spoke.

A flash of...something passed over Lottie's face, or maybe I imagined it, because then she smiled – her dimples fully indented.

"Yes, of course. He's coming straight from the airport. He's been skiing."

"Great. At least I'll know one other person."

Will and Kyle had met when Kyle came over for a few days last Christmas – that incredible last year of college before we'd been ripped apart and put on different slipstreams towards the big scary bad that was adulthood.

They'd instantly bonded over the weird bands they both loved and spent many a night chatting in old man pubs. Oli had got on well with Kyle too. Speaking of which, I hadn't seen him in aaaaages.

The doorbell went.

"I'll get it!" Lottie yelled, smushing her now-empty plastic cup onto the table. "You get the music going."

She dashed to the door and Kyle and I shrugged at each other, before turning the volume up.

"You need to tell them," he said again.

"I will, I will." I picked out The Smiths so everyone at the party would think I was cooler than I actually am.

I'd started to wonder if Lottie would even *mind* when I told her my news.

Everyone was here! Everyone, everyone. All the old FemSoc lot, some of The Imposters, a band we knew, and people from college and people I'd grown up with and who just knew me as Lottie, rather than that up-herself girl. The only shitter was that Megan wasn't here. But as she was on a beach in Thailand having the most epic time of her life, I couldn't feel too bummed about it.

I was swirling and twirling and hugging everyone – jumping with excitement as each new face made it through the door. It felt so nice and safe and comfortable, like my old pair of pyjama bottoms where the butt has almost worn through. The music thumped the walls, bottles clanged and crashed as they were unloaded in the kitchen, the ping-and-hiss of dozens of opening beer cans littered the air.

Still no message from Will though…

He was supposed to have landed half an hour ago. And according to the real-time information on my phone, the plane had, indeed, landed on time. Which is a shocking amount of stalkerness on my part. But this is what happens to me if I have a boyfriend and he comes for the night and doesn't have sex with me. I turn into activate-the-psycho.

But it was fine, because here was another glass of wine. Just one more couldn't hurt, could it? I drink wine in London all the time because it's the only drink you can afford really. Me and the few people off my Philosophy, Politics and Economics course who I've managed to win over go to a Bargain Booze down the road to stockpile, and then drink wine around one of theirs. I've also noticed Heather, Aimee and Jade doing this on numerous occasions. Sometimes they've actually invited me to join in, but only in a really hollow, false way that's made it clear they'd be devastated if I actually said yes.

"Maybe you should just say yes," Will had said. "They're not that bad."

"Will, have you not met them? They literally flinch whenever I mention feminism," I replied. "That's if they're not already rolling their eyes. Once, Heather, flinched and rolled her eyes at the same time while applying her false eyelashes, which is quite an achievement. She wears false eyelashes every single day, Will. All three of them do. Every. Single. Day. And they dressed up as Playboy Bunnies in Freshers' Week. Playboy. Bunnies. And they're friends with some guys from the rugby team, who make actual rape jokes, and my housemates laugh at them!"

"God, I know, I know. You've told me already," Will said. Before he didn't have sex with me.

Now I was hugging Ethan, a guy we knew from college. And I found I kept talking about London. Utter freaking nonsense about it, to make up for all the conflicting thoughts in my head.

"Yeah, the energy there is just so...unlike anything I've ever felt before." Why was I using the word "energy"? I don't usually use the word "energy". "And there was this one time, when we stayed up all night, and we walked past St Paul's Cathedral as the sun was rising. I mean, you don't get a better walk home after a night out than that, right?"

Ethan nodded, looking over my head.

"Where's Evie?" he asked.

That was a point. Where WAS Evie? She should've been here by now. Whenever Now is. I wasn't sure of the time. It must be nearly midnight already, right?

I turned, without saying goodbye, to look for her. She wasn't in the packed kitchen. She wasn't sitting on the stairs with the people playing guitar and singing Tenacious D. She wasn't dancing in the living room with Sylvia, who was waaaaay more drunk than me already, which was quite frankly a relief. Deflection drunkenness is the way forward. I spotted Amber, chatting with some of the Art Lot in the hallway, and tapped her hard on the shoulder.

"Oww, what is it, Lottie?"

"Where's Evie?"

"Have you not seen your phone? She said she's running late."

I pulled out my phone. TWO MESSAGES. Yes! One from Evie, saying she was late, and one from Will.

On my way.

No kiss.

On my way no kiss.

No kiss.

First no sex and then no kiss.

Where was the wine again?

I sat on the floor, Oli still on the bed. I'm not sure why I was on the carpet, but I think I just sort of wilted onto it.

Also, Oli kept punching his pillow and it was starting to scare me.

BAD THOUGHT

Why is he being so selfish? You've been with him all day.

BAD THOUGHT

You knew he'd do this.

"Oli, stop punching the pillow. Please." I tried to use the tone of voice that *I'd* found helpful when I spiralled. Firm but warm, in-control but kind. My coat was still on, my bag still on my arm, but I knew I wouldn't be leaving for a while. Not when he was like this. Oli did one extra punch and then flopped face down onto the bed and started to cry. Tears scratched my own eyes but I blinked like mad to stop them. Seeing me cry only made him worse. I got up and perched gingerly on the bed, stroking his back, wondering once again how only moments ago we'd been tangled in a compromising clinch. Him smiling and confident and sexy...until it came to people who weren't him and their ability to leave the house.

He looked up, his eyes wet and red.

VERY BAD UNFEMINIST THOUGHT

I don't like seeing boys cry.

And I wanted to slap myself. And him. Or to throw myself on the pillow and cry too. And scream and act out all the emotions I felt about what was happening and how bloody unfair it all was.

"I'm sorry," he said. "I'm sorry. I'm so sorry. You should just break up with me. You don't deserve this in your life."

"Stop being stupid." I reached out to stroke his cheek but stopped myself at the last moment, remembering. I touched his shoulder instead.

"I just...just...don't want you to go."

I bit my lip. "I know that."

"But I know it's not fair of me to ask you to stay."

BAD THOUGHT

But you're asking anyway...

"No...it's not." My voice was firmer and I saw him harden. Like I used to whenever people were firm with me. Even though you know it's for your own good. Even though they're only following the instructions of the medical professionals Who Know Best. Even though, logically, you know it hurts them to be this firm just as much as it hurts you.

"It's just...just...it's so unfair."

And secretly I thought, *I know*. And not just unfair for you.

What happened with Oli

We were supposed to be having a happily-ever-after. Ever since that night at his eighteenth birthday party – when he grabbed my hand and pulled me to one side and kissed me. We'd both worked so hard to get there. After my OCD relapse, every inch of recovery I'd made felt like crawling over an acre of glass shards. Oli was in recovery too – though he was way ahead of me. We'd been advised not to date, not like we were in any fit state to anyway.

Slowly, I got better, and Oli got more better. I went back to college, I managed to lower my dosage to just under five mil, which felt like enough to keep The Crazy at bay, but low enough that I felt like me again. Then his birthday happened and everything fell into place. I fell in love like salt dissolving in warm water – all my bitterness and unhappiness fading away into clear.

I should've known that just because it looks clear, doesn't mean the bitterness isn't still there.

We both started at the same local university in September. He did Film Studies, and I surprised everyone by taking Psychology.

And then – how do I put it?

I flew. Oli sank.

It was like two different winds had blown us onto two totally different paths.

I loved uni. I loved it from the first day. I was, naturally, terrified. By all the new people, by the fact there's an actual thing called "Freshers' Flu". I worried that people would think I was a weirdo for still living at home rather than in halls. But I was determined not to let my fear ruin this, like it had my first year of college. I went to every social, joined three different societies, drank and danced and spent most of my student loan on late-night taxis home.

Oli was determined too.

Oli's sinking was nothing to do with how determined he was not to sink.

Life's just a bitch sometimes.

We've talked, so much, about what triggered his relapse. Even after everything we've been through and learned, we still want to crowbar in a reasonable narrative, a smidgen of logic into *why* a brain will randomly misbehave. But really, all that happened was one day Oli was fine, then one morning – a month into term – he woke up and found he couldn't leave the house.

Oli hasn't left the house since that morning.

He's dropped out of uni. He's essentially dropped off the face of any earth that isn't the walls that enclose him. The therapist has to come to his house for his sessions. Even after *two months*, he has not left the house.

And I don't know what to do.

I was always so worried about my own potential to relapse. Of my own tendency to butt-slide down into the centre of Crazy Canyon. It never occurred to me Oli could slide and I wouldn't.

I was always the one who slid.

On my good days, all I feel is horribly sad. That this has happened to him, that this is impacting us. On my bad days, I feel angry. Angry at him for doing this to me. To us. Angry at him for not being stronger. Angry at the world for not just leaving us the hell alone. Angry that his relapse is ruining my first year of university – making me rush back to check he's okay when I should be out having fun and enjoying being a fresher. Angry at myself for being such a heartless, selfish bitch for even thinking such a thing. Worried that somehow his relapse is contagious. On my lower days, when I've been kept up all night by his frantic messages, I'll find myself buying into his anxieties, thinking, *Oh God, maybe you're right. Maybe it* is *unsafe outside, maybe I should copy you.* And I have to ring my new adult therapist and talk it through with her until I feel okay again.

More than anything, like Oli said, it just feels unfair.

"You know I love you?" I said. "That I can love you and still go to this party?"

He half-nodded, his eyes narrowing, even though I could see he didn't want them to. "I just can't believe I won't get to be with my girlfriend at midnight."

It did suck. I know it's stupid and superficial and New Year's Eve is a big bunch of baloney, but it did suck.

"It's not like I'm going to kiss anyone else."

"You should." He crossed his arms. "You should go and find someone NORMAL."

"You know there's no such thing as normal…"

"And you know that's bullshit and normal people leave the house," he replied.

BAD THOUGHT

Maybe if you just TRIED to leave the house?

BAD THOUGHT

For God's sake, Evie. Do you not remember what it feels like? When did you become such an unfeeling bitch?

"Look, Oli. You'll get there. You know rushing yourself won't help."

He looked up at me with his basilly green eyes. That were so very basilly that sometimes I thought he could cry into tomato sauce and it would taste nicer.

"Why are you so good at this?"

"At what?"

"At not making me feel like a dysfunctional arsehole."

BAD THOUGHT

Because I don't say what I actually think...

I held his hand, entwining my fingers through his,

squeezing the webbing until it almost hurt. "Because I've been there. I get it, remember?"

"I know… You're doing so well, Evie. I'm so proud. I just wish I wasn't ruining how well you're doing…"

"You're not ruining—"

"I am. I know you're never going to admit it, but I am."

He was. Not that I'd ever tell him. About the sag I felt in my tummy when I had to leave a night out early. Or the way I had to keep lying to everyone, because he didn't want anyone else to know he'd "failed". His words, not mine.

But I loved him. So that made it okay hopefully. And he was right, I'd never admit it.

My phone buzzed. Lottie.

WHERE IN THE NAME OF BUDDHA'S ARSE ARE YOU? IF YOU DON'T GET HERE SOON I'M GOING TO TURN INTO A PUMPKIN AT MIDNIGHT.

Oli read it over my shoulder. "I guess you should get going," he said, in a sad way.

My phone buzzed again.

A SEXY PUMPKIN.

We both giggled, him nuzzling his head into my shoulder. I took a deep breath and smelled his smell, letting its familiarity calm me.

"I'll call you at midnight?" I stood up, still holding his hand.

"You might have trouble getting through."

"Well, I can try..."

I kissed him once more. He tried to pull me down again, to get me into a deeper kiss, and I knew it was to keep me there longer.

Not that he meant it that way. Well, he did. But it's not like he was proud of it.

"I really should go. I don't want Lottie to turn into a sexy pumpkin. Whatever that is anyway..."

"Tell the girls I said hi."

I pulled my coat around myself. It looked freezing outside – the sky full of stars, no clouds to keep any heat in. I liked the air cold. It felt clean and crisp and germless. I turned for the door, feeling a knife blade of guilt stab me in the guts with every step. But I had to go. I couldn't not live. Lottie, Amber and I never got any time together any more – Lottie especially. This was the first time she'd visited since she went to London and everyone had been so busy with Christmas we'd not really got to hang out much.

I held the door frame just before leaving and turned.

"I love you, you know that, right?" I said. Because I did. I really did.

Oli gave me his sad smile. The one that I knew meant he'd dissolve the moment I walked out the door – spiralling and blaming himself and hating himself and all other sorts of unpleasantries that come from a brain that is more bully than brain.

What therapy says

But that doesn't mean you should stay.
It's actually worse for him if you stay...

"I know. I love you too, Evie."

"Happy New Year, I guess."

His eyes were so sad. Like all the basil had wilted and died. "Yeah, happy New Year, I guess."

9 O'CLOCK

amber

Lottie has been sick down my fucking wall.

I would kill her dead. But even in her complete drunken state she actually managed to stagger into the back garden, so at least she was only sick down an exterior wall… So I'd only strangle her until she lost consciousness but let her live.

"Lottie?" I'd stepped out into the dark air, looking around for her. She'd disappeared from the party after yelling at anyone who'd listen about how "AMAAAZING" London was.

It was quieter outside, the music only a dull metallic

thump-thumping. Luckily the cold was keeping people inside the house, so Penny's prize olive tree collection wasn't at risk.

That's when I heard the vomiting. I turned and saw her leaning against the wall, being sick neatly down it. But still – being sick down my fucking wall.

"Lottie?"

She stopped, almost like my voice commanded it, and looked up like nothing had happened at all.

"AMBER!" She grinned. "Wonderful to see you, just wonderful."

Christ, how was she *this* wasted? Lottie never really used to get wasted. Apart from that one night at Oli's eighteenth.

"You've been sick."

She wiped her mouth. "No I haven't."

"Lottie, I just saw you being sick."

"That is not sick. That's a…a…just something I ate disagreeing with me."

"That's what vomit is. That's literally what vomit is."

She stumbled on nothing, catching herself mid-fall

and straightening herself up. "Ahh, relax, Amber. Take a pill of the chill. I'll clean it up, just CALM DOWN, DEAR." And she started laughing hysterically.

I used to love drunk Lottie. She was random, charming… But today…tonight…she'd just been sick on my wall. Dad was going to freak.

As if on cue, my phone went. Vibrating madly in my hand – Dad's number.

"Shit," I whispered. "Lottie, please clean it up." I turned and walked as far down the garden as I could so Dad wouldn't hear the loud music.

"Hi, Dad," I said, loudly.

"Hey, Amber." His voice was slightly slurred and cheery. They were an hour ahead in their skiing place. "I just thought I'd say happy New Year before the phones all jam up."

I smiled in the darkness. "Are you drunk, Dad?"

"I may've had a few après-skis, yes."

"Well, happy New Year!"

"Yes, poppet. What are you and young Kyle up to?" He always did that, called him "young Kyle" – diminishing any seriousness about him. Even though Kyle was twenty-one now.

"Ahh, you know. Just chilling with some films. We might turn on Jools Holland closer to midnight – Kyle loves him."

Just then a huge crash emanated from the garden shed.

"What was that?" Dad asked.

"Oh, sorry, that's Kyle." I made my voice even louder. "He's just…erm…clattering with the dishes, trying to find the deep one so we can make nachos."

"Riiight."

I could feel the thump of the music under the gravel, but there was music blasting down Dad's line too.

"How's Penny and Craig?"

"They're good, they're good. Craig's been…well… the exercise is good for him. And Penny's loving the spa. It's weird not having you here with us," Dad started. "I…guess we need to start getting used to it."

My tummy squidged. "I'm still here for a while. I've got to finish my foundation course first."

"I know, I know." He gulped. "But, well, this year. It's going to be the year we lose you..."

My throat caught, and I took a big breath to try and dislodge the lump. "You're not losing me," I said for, like, the eighteenth time since I got the news. "I'm only a plane ride away, and there'll be holidays."

"Still though, Amber..." A pause; I heard the hesitation in his voice too. "It's far."

"It's a really good art school."

"I know, and we're so proud of you, poppet. It's just... well...anyway, enjoy your film. I just wanted to say happy New Year."

There was a disturbance in the background. I heard Penny: "*Come on, Brian, I need another drink.*"

"Happy New Year," I yelled, wanting to be heard over Penny. Still, after all this time, feeling like I was in a competition with her that I always lost.

"Yes...yes...what drink do you want, gorgeous? Bye, Ambe..." The line went dead. The noise of my party – and some weird tinkling sound – the only things left ringing in my ears.

"Bye," I said, to no one.

I was leaving.

I was leaving home. I was leaving the country.

And it suddenly hit me just what that meant.

This house, this tiny town, my friends, the Spinster Club – I'd be leaving all of it. My stomach flipped again, my breath getting faster. I'd said yes, I'd made my decision. But the decision still regurgitated on me, like when you eat too much melted Camembert in one go and do cheese burps for two days afterwards.

It had, oddly enough, been my mum's idea for me to apply for American art school. "*The camp is doing well and we wanted to do something for you...*" *Do something* meant *pay the extortionate American college fees* so I could go to art school over there. I think she expected me to pick a school in California, near her, but then I found out that Rhode Island School of Design is right next to Brown – right next to Kyle. And, even though it makes me the worst feminist in the world, that's what made me apply. Because – there's no undramatic way to put this – Kyle is my guts. Kyle is my family. He's my insides. He is home.

He, oddly enough, initially didn't like the idea.

"You can't leave your country to come be with me," was Kyle's first reaction.

"Why not? Are you planning to break up with me or something?"

He sighed and pulled my head into his chest, rubbing my hair with his fist like I was a child. "Shut it, you," he said, in his naff English accent. "You KNOW that's not it. I just don't want to be the reason you give up your life. You've got to do this for you, not for me, not for us. I love you too much to watch you leave everything just for me."

"But you say such lovely things, like that!"

It had been summer. I'd gone to stay with him and his "folks" in their tiny mountain town outside Yosemite. His parents and his many, many siblings had made me feel like family instantly. My insides still radiated from the warmth of it. He'd pulled his computer over and started typing.

"What are you doing?"

"Actually researching this art school, so you can start wanting this for you…"

After an hour on the website, I was smitten. Rhode Island School of Design was everything I wanted out of an art school. I could just see myself there – with American friends, learning how to make amazing art. Kyle even got us cheap flights to go over for two days so I could wander around the empty campus and see how I liked it.

I liked it. I loved it even…

That's when he smiled and said, "And now you have my permission to apply," and I'd hit him.

I'd been scared I wouldn't get in, that I didn't have enough of a portfolio yet after only a month of art college. But I sent off fifteen paintings and filled out all the forms and crossed every part of my body it's possible to cross. And, two weeks ago, I got an acceptance letter. I couldn't stop smiling. It was like my cheeks were permanently stretched that way. Mum had screamed down the phone, with what appeared to be genuine joy and delight. Dad had looked forlorn but managed to say, "It's an incredible opportunity, Amber." Penny had said, hollowly, "Oh, but, Amber, we'll miss you so much," and it was so false-sounding I'm surprised parts of her didn't crumble in on themselves. I'd told everyone at art college, and they all thought it was cool. I'd even told Whinnie, my friend from camp, who did a victory dance over Skype before yelling "ROAD TRIIIIP!" and booking me in for several weekends in Albuquerque despite it being a year away.

I'd told everyone really – apart from Evie and Lottie. My supposed best friends.

I just couldn't bring myself to do it somehow. We'd split apart so much already, in a heartbreaking, horrific way that I never could've dreamed possible. Even though Evie was still living close, we didn't see a huge amount of each other. She kept cancelling plans last minute with flimsy excuses. She spent a lot of time with Oli, but never invited him along so we could all hang out. And, Lottie, well...I couldn't figure out what the hell was going on with Lottie.

Speaking of which, I heard a shriek and another clatter. I ran back to the house and found Lottie on the ground, wrestling with my garden hose, which was spraying her everywhere with water.

"Turn it off, turn it off!"

I ran to the tap and spun it until the water stopped. Lottie lay on her back, half her body drenched. Then she started laughing.

"AhahaHAHHAHAHAHAHAHA, THE HOSE IS WET. THE HOSE. THE HOSE." She held her arms up like a child and I sighed and pulled her upright.

"What are you doing with the hose?"

"I was washing off the sick I definitely didn't do!"

I looked behind her at the wall where her vom had so recently been. It had gone – though it was probably now just diluted into the puddle under my feet. She looked so brazen and proud of herself and soggy that I couldn't help but smile… She smiled back, shivering, her eyes not quite focusing. I felt a rush of sudden love for her, even though she was pissed and annoying and kept droning on about London. I realized I…missed her.

"You're mental, you know that?"

"Who's mental?" Evie called, as she appeared at the door. "Who's ripping off my brand?"

"EVIE!" we both yelled, running over to hug her with a big ooomph.

"Oww, Lottie, why are you so wet?"

"I'm not wet, you're just dry." Lottie hugged us harder.

"Ouch, Amber, you're really working your biceps into this thing," Evie said.

"Whoops, sorry." I had got into the hug a bit too much, feeling sad and wonderful at us all being together. "I just felt the love."

The hug broke off too soon as Lottie's moistness seeped into my and Evie's outfits. "How's it going? Is Oli okay?" I asked, catching Lottie who'd stumbled on thin air.

"Umm." Evie's face clammed up. Yikes, what was going on there? "Yeah, it's all good. I mean, he's got a cold, so he can't come tonight but…oh, Lottie, Will is inside."

"WILL?" Lottie didn't even say goodbye. She just careered through the patio doors, and got swallowed by the party.

"Aaaand there she goes." Evie smiled, though her

smile wasn't her real smile. It was her tense teeth-gritted *no-I'm-fine-honestly* smile. "It's freezing out here, can we go back into the party?"

I was about to ask what was up but she'd hurried inside.

"Yep, sure," I said to no one, following her in. "I need to check the place isn't being trashed anyway."

Kyle seemed to have kept everything under control. People filled everywhere – cluttering up the stairs, perching on the edges of tables and sofas, clutching plastic cups, yelling to each other to be heard over the music. But no one – bar Lottie and Sylvia – seemed too wasted or troublesome. Lottie was nowhere to be seen anyway, nor Will.

"Hey, where have you guys been?" Kyle tucked me under his arm, kissing my face. "I'm teaching people the wonder of beer pong."

"Hopefully in a place where there is no carpet?" I asked.

"Of course, of course, it's in the kitchen. Wanna game?"

Evie and I raised our eyebrows at each other.

"We're in."

lottie

I'm not drunk, you're drunk.

Woahhhh. This party is BRILLIANT. Everyone, like EVERYONE is here. From my past. My happy wonderful past. Where I was the kick-ass girl who spawned the Vagilante campaign. Not the prudish housemate everyone laughs about in the kitchen.

I am in the kitchen. Because that's where the wine is.

And I am drinking the wine.

I mean – it is New Year's EVE. Festival of the…umm… somethingorothers. It's, like, against TRADITION not to have a few drinks on a day as historic as that.

I am rambling at someone. But they seem intrigued. Maybe because I am propping myself up on their shoulder.

"I mean, *Home Alone*," I am saying. "Mad, isn't it? Stupid Macaulay Culkin. And, like, why was it up to the MUM to give a shit about her son maybe getting murdered in their family home? The dad is all like JUST CALM DOWN, DEAR, but their kid COULD DIE." Ethan is grinning at my hand being on his shoulder. I only just realized I'm talking to Ethan again. *You should stop touching him, you have a boyfriend*, is a thought that just came into my head. Or did it? I can't remember thoughts. "Also" – I'm really leaning on Ethan – "who doesn't like toppings on their pizza? I mean what the heck is wrong with Kevin in *Home Alone* anyway? He only likes cheese pizza! What is the POINT of pizza if you don't have any toppings?"

Laughter, there's laughter. And then Ethan is gone and I'm holding the table to keep myself upright. Not because I'm drunk. Just because my arm needs proper support to give my body proper support. That's just PHYSICS.

Where is Will? Why isn't he here yet? Why was there no kiss in the message and no sex in my uni bedroom? I do not like feeling this way. Needy and worried and jumpy. Leap leap leaping out of my skin the moment my phone goes. Will never usually makes me feel like this. Will and I. Me and Will. Lottie and Will. Will and Lottie. We are A Good Couple. He is so nice and strong and good for me and good in bed that he's made me stay in a relationship for a YEAR. A whole year of my prime experimentation years. Yes, being in different unis is hard. Everyone says that – all smug and knowing-it-all – but we're managing, aren't we?

OOOH BEER PONG. KYLE IS HERE AND HE'S STARTED A GAME OF BEER PONG.

I'm not very good at beer pong…

No, I don't feel sick. YOU feel sick. I don't get sick. I'm just outside because you need fresh air sometimes. And, look, here is this wall, I may just lean against it and spit a little bit because sometimes you need to spit.

"Lottie?"

Amber! Amber is here.

Oh bollocks, she's angry. She always seems angry with me these days. Not that I see her much these days. I'm telling her it will be fine. Because it will be fine. Everything is fine. I'm fine. Uni is fine. Our friendship is fine. Will is fine. We are fine. The vomit on the wall which I'm sure isn't mine is fine. Well, maybe it's a bit mine. But it's more spit than vomit.

Amber's stormed off now, leaving me here in the dark and cold.

It's very dark and cold in the dark and cold.

I know! I'll make her happy! I'll clean the vomit off the wall and then she'll be thankful and then we can get back to how we used to be because even though, yes, I've had a bit of wine I can tell things aren't how they used to be.

Which is sad.

So sad that I'm crying a little bit in this shed I've found.

That may also be a bit to do with the fact I've pronged my bum with a garden fork.

Ouch.

Bum hurts.

Hose! Here's the hose.

I'm not drunk because drunk people totally can't attach a freaking hose to a garden tap and that is something I've just done totally unaided.

Splish splash splosh. All the vom is coming off the wall nicely.

Hang on, why is the hose spraying me?

IT'S SO WET OH MY GOD IT'S WET AND COLD AND SLIPPERY…AHH I'M ON THE FLOOR AND I'M SO WET AND FREEZING FREEZING.

Amber! Amber is here and she's helping! And smiling!

The water has gone. Every inch of my skin is an icicle but the water has gone. And Evie is here. Evie! I love Evie. She's so good and brave and strong. What a lovely hug. God, I love these girls. Why have we let things get weird? We have to mend things. I know! We'll blow off the party and go upstairs and have a Spinster Club meeting, like old times. It will be brilliant. It's just what I need. I miss them. I need them back. Why have they even gone? This hug is so nice.

Hang on? Did Evie just say Will is here?

I need to find Will.

The party is busy, people everywhere. Oh, there's the beer pong! I wasn't very good at the beer pong. No Will there though. There is Ethan again. He has just reached his arm around my waist, trying to pull me into him.

"Don't be sleazy!" I push him off.

Maybe he's swearing at me as I walk away. I'm not sure, the music is loud.

Bash bash bash goes the music. My mouth tastes of sick a little bit.

No Will in the living room. But Jane is there. WITHOUT JOEL. Duh duh DUHHHHHH. She dumped him after she went off to uni, I heard. Found some other guy to dedicate her entire life to. Whoops. That was mean. I'm not supposed to be mean about Jane. It upsets Evie. No Will downstairs. Up the stairs I go.

OWWWW FELL OVER ON THE STUPID STAIRS.

Stupid stairs. What are they doing there? Where is Will? All these people in the corridor, in my way. For some reason they keep asking, "Lottie, are you okay?"

And there, there is Will. I can see his blond hair and the glint of his glasses. His little head in Amber's parents' room, where people are sitting around playing poker.

"WILL!" I announce my arrival, leaning against the door to try and look sexy and also, for some reason, because I'm not very good at standing up properly right now.

Will looks up and it makes my heart hurt. I missed him. I really missed him. I love his little face. Even if it looks pissed off, or maybe I'm imagining that.

"Lottie." He stands up and begins stepping over the poker game delicately to get to me. "I couldn't find you."

I have a thought. *Why did he not look harder? Why did he arrive and start playing poker and not try and find me harder?* But I push it away and launch myself at him. I jump into his arms and wrap my legs around him, which always looks damn amazing in the films. But Will isn't ready or prepared or Channing Tatum so he buckles under my weight and we fall to the floor, me on top of him.

Everyone is laughing and applauding and yelling "OH MY GOD, FA-IL!" while Will tips me off him, his glasses all askew and says, "Jesus, Lottie, *how drunk are you?*" He scrambles to stand up, then looks down at himself…and the wet stains on his shirt. "Why are you soaking wet?"

"I missed you!" I say, still on the floor, struggling to stand. "Did you miss me? How was skiing? Why are you being weird with me?"

My arm. He's holding my arm. Leading me out of the room, down the hallway.

"Lottie, jeez, why are you so wasted?"

I cross my arms. "I'm not wasted, you're wasted." He sighs and runs his hands through his hair, while I just stand there. Almost on the verge of tears.

"Why didn't you have sex with me?"

"What? I mean, what?"

Why did I say that? Why did that come out? We didn't even really say hello. And straight in I go, into the bad stuff. Will is frowning. He always seems to be frowning.

"When you came over to mine?" Is my voice that

slurry? I can hardly understand myself. "You didn't have sex with me. And then you just messaged and you didn't put a kiss and...and...and..." Oh no...the vomit... there's more vomit to come... No no, not here, not with Will here, looking at me like that. "...and...HANG ON A MOMENT."

Running. Running to the bathroom. Knock knocking. Yelling, "Let me in." Door opens. Run inside. Fall to knees. Be sick.

Sick again.

And again.

Ouch my throat hurts.

Will here. Holding my hair back.

Saying nice things.

Also saying, "Lottie, what the hell is going on?"

Stopped being sick now.

Just crying. Not sure why I'm crying. But I am.

Will's hand rubbing my back. "Come on, Lottie. There's a queue outside."

Trying to pick myself up off the floor. "Did you miss me, Will? When you were away?"

His hands under my armpits, pulling me up. "Come on, up you come."

"Why did you laugh with my housemates? You know they're not nice to me."

Gently guiding me into Amber's room, if the smell of oil paints is anything to go by. "I think you need a lie-down."

"Will? Will?"

"Shh shh. Just sleep it off a bit. I'll wake you before midnight."

Getting under Amber's covers. Can smell Amber's perfume on them.

"Will? What's going on? With you and me. Something is going on."

And even through my drunken haze, I see something cross his face. A wince. One he suppresses instantly.

"Lottie, not tonight. It's New Year's Eve. Shh. Just lie back, have a nap."

"I DON'T WANT A NAP, I WANT YOU TO TELL ME WHAT'S GOING ON."

But the bed really is very soft. And the duvet really

is very warm. And the pillow really is very sinky. And I really am very cold from being wet. And my throat really is very sore. And my head really is very heavy.

And Will is stroking my hair. And he wouldn't stroke my hair if he didn't still love me, would he? And…and…

…and…

The walk to the party was beyond cold. I almost wanted the ability to remove my arms from their sockets, just so I could wrap them around myself further. The streets buzzed and fizzed with New Year energy – hollow thuds of music echoing as I walked past people's houses, pissed-up merrymakers stumbling across the pavement wearing novelty headbands. I felt a rush of annoyance at Lottie all of a sudden, thinking, *See, our little town isn't so bad. Yes, it's not London, but it's got something.* But I pushed it away. Unlike Amber, I like to give people the benefit of the doubt, and I could sense Lottie's London boasting might not be coming from the happiest of places. I was willing to give her these holidays to hopefully tell us as much.

Or maybe I was just an idiot. Friendships die. They die every day. People grow up and grow apart and the threads holding you together snap or fall to the floor and all you're left with are bittersweet memories.

URGENT THOUGHT

You can't lose those girls. Not now.

BAD THOUGHT

So why aren't you telling them about Oli?

It was too cold to get my phone out but I could feel it buzzing in my pocket.

I knew what the messages would say anyway...

I heard Amber's party before I turned the corner. The Dixie Chicks' wails echoed down her cul-de-sac. I smiled. She must still be in control of the playlist.

"Boys always take over the playlists at parties, have you ever noticed?" Amber had complained to me. "It's never a girl aggressively plugging in her phone, assuming they can do better. God, feminism is everywhere, even at parties, isn't it?"

Clumps of shivering smokers lined her garden path as I walked up to the door, nodding hello to some people I recognized from college. Everyone looked slightly different – sporting a new haircut, or piercing, or article of clothing I wouldn't have ever seen them in at college. Uni was changing all of us – giving us the chance to carve out new identities, free from the suffocating fumes of growing up in a small town where Who You Are is settled on so young, labels sticking to you with reinforced superglue. Even I was enjoying my second rendition of not being *the-girl-who-went-nuts*.

I pushed through the front door and the party swallowed me whole, my ears instantly ringing with the music, my fringe getting sweaty with the warmth of so many people. I stood on tiptoe to try and find anyone I knew, but couldn't see over all the heads. I'd just have to ferret around people's ankles like bloody always.

But first – my phone.

I waited outside the downstairs loo, trying not to think about how many different people of different drunk and hygiene levels had already used it that evening. The lock scraped back and a girl from Amber's art class last year smiled as she stepped to one side. She smelled nice, of perfume, and had flushed the loo, so it wasn't as bad as I'd thought.

I wrapped my hand in tissue, then used it to put the seat down, sitting on the loo like it was a chair.

Five messages.

All from Oli.

Hey, I'm sorry about earlier.

I'm really sorry.

I didn't mean to send two messages, sorry. Have a good night.

How's the party?

I'm sorry I can't be there.

I sighed, my eyes prickling as I read them all.

BAD THOUGHT

Honestly, Oli. I just got here!

BAD THOUGHT

Why is he being so needy? Why can't he just let me enjoy the party?

BAD THOUGHT

If you don't reply straight away he might spiral.

I lifted my head to the ceiling, feeling panic and claustrophobia creep in, invading my brain. Taking over.

BAD THOUGHT

You're not going to be able to handle this, Evie.

BAD THOUGHT

But you can't break up with him, Evie.
Then what will he do?

Deep breaths. In for five, out for seven. In for five, out for seven. *Only send one message back.* In for five, out for seven. *Otherwise you're just buying into his anxiety.*

In for five, out for seven. *That's what the therapist said.* In for five, out for seven. *It may seem cruel, but it's what's best for him.* In for five, out for seven. In for...

I jumped at the loud knock at the door.

"ARE YOU DOING A MASSIVE SHIT IN THERE OR SOMETHING?"

Oh God... "Sorry, just a second!"

I punched in a reply.

I love you, stop saying sorry. I'll speak to you at midnight.

Then opened the door to find Will.

"Will!"

"Evie." His eyes were bloodshot beneath his glasses.

"I wasn't doing a poo. I was just on my phone."

"Nice to see you too." He laughed. "I really need the loo though. I came straight from the airport."

"Oh okay." I stepped aside to let him past. "You seen Lottie? I only just got here."

Will's face scrunched up, only for a second before

he recovered, but still. Enough for me to snuffle out something was wrong. Oh God, I hoped Lottie and him were okay. I'd only just got around to liking him.

"Nope, can't find her. I really need to pee now." He was still smiling as he closed the door, but he was still closing the door.

I explored the rest of the party, looking everywhere for Amber and Lottie. I needed them. I needed to just laugh with them and be with them and for them to take the piss out of me and make me forget all the scary stuff that was happening with Oli. I stumbled across Kyle, hosting a giant game of beer pong in the kitchen. He got very excited by me – picking me up like a toy and swirling me around the room, his breath smelling of beer.

"EVIE BUDDY, YOU MADE IT."

He really was so very wonderful and American. He put me down when I asked him to and directed me to the garden.

"Amber's outside. Probably on the phone to her dad, I think. Trying to convince him she's not having a party."

And there, as I stepped out into the darkness, there they were. Lottie soaking wet for some unknown reason. We all hugged, Lottie getting her wetness all over me and in that moment I relaxed. Even though I could feel my phone vibrating through my coat pocket. They were here, after this weird term, we were all together again. I felt…whole. Well, I did until Lottie found out Will'd arrived and vanished like a magic trick.

Amber asked how Oli was.

My throat clammed up.

BAD THOUGHT

You can't tell her.

She'll tell you to break up with him.

BAD THOUGHT

And maybe you want to hear that.

WORSE THOUGHT

Because you're struggling with this, Evie.
You're really struggling.

So, when we went inside and Kyle came over again, sweeping Amber up into his wonderful arms, and challenged us to a game of beer pong, the only thought I had was…

Might as well.

10 O'CLOCK

amber

So, I'm not very good at beer pong.

"It's not fair," I said. "I swear I'm only this bad because I'm tall and therefore further away from the table."

I aimed, took a shot, and then got the ball right into one of Evie's red cups.

The crowd surrounding us cheered and started chanting, "*Chug it, chug it, chug it.*"

Evie desperately picked up the red cup and tipped her head back, getting a lot of it down her nice black dress.

"I'M AMAZING AT BEER PONG," I declared.

Evie wiped her mouth, and took her turn. She squinted, fierce concentration on her face, her eyes narrowed, she let go of the ball and...and...

...bollocks, it plopped right into one of my cups.

The crowd went crazy. *CHUGCHUGCHUGCHUG.* I had no choice but to pick up the cup and down the beer inside. At least it was only beer.

Kyle, the sensible but wonderful man that he is, says it's imperative you always keep it to beer pong, rather than gin or vodka pong, "Otherwise sick most definitely will end up on your parents' carpet and they'll get me deported."

Kyle leaned in, his breath tickling my ear. "I think we should concede, gorgeous. Otherwise we're both going to be too wasted to look after all the other wasted people."

"That is a very fair and valid point."

I raised my hands in surrender and everyone groaned. "I have to make sure you don't all trash the place," I protested.

Evie leaped into the air in triumph. "I won a game!

I won beer pong. I am the QUEEN OF BEER PONG. I AM MASTER AND CHAMPION OF THE PONG UNIVERSE OF THE BEER VARIETY."

"You," Kyle called over the table, "are quite drunk."

"Not another one," I said. "Lottie's bad enough."

That was a point. Where *was* Lottie? I hadn't seen her in ages, and Lottie is not the sort of person you can miss at parties. I decided to go on a hunt for her. I also needed to check my house wasn't getting wrecked.

Dancing had started in the living room. In my beer pongingness, some twat guy had taken over my playlist and now heavy house music burst from the speakers. I hated it, but the lads pogoing around the sofas didn't seem to share my sentiment. The hallway was lined with people holding the red plastic cups Kyle had insisted on and catching up on each other's gossip.

"So, in Sheffield, there's this one club night where, like, drinks are only eighty pence."

"That's nothing. In my halls in Leeds, you can get a quadruple vodka and Coke for a pound. I saw them cleaning the toilets with the vodka at one point though..."

That was one thing I'd noticed since people had started returning to our hometown this Christmas – everyone was in a constant competition over who was at the best uni. And that was *nothing* to the competition between the people who had gone to uni and the people who'd stayed home for whatever reason. I couldn't pretend that those who had gone off hadn't come back... smugger. Acting like they were all worldly just because they'd stolen a traffic cone while dressed as a smurf. Maybe it just didn't rub off on me because I wasn't at uni yet – art people always have to do foundation years to build their portfolio. Or maybe it was because I was about to put an entire ocean between me and home, rather than just a section of the M1. Whatever. It didn't really bother me, apart from the fact Lottie had appeared to buy into it – constantly droning on about London.

Lottie...

Where the heck had she gone?

Everyone – predictably – had stamped over the passive-aggressive piece of string I'd hung across the top of the stairs, asking them to stay on the ground floor.

I spotted Jane, who was dressed all differently, chatting to a very drunk Sylvia and said hi.

"You seen Lottie?"

They both shook their heads. "Though, have you heard?" Jane asked. "She has her own COLUMN at her student newspaper. She's only a fresher. The other students must HATE her."

That thought hadn't occurred to me about Lottie and her column, though I guess it made sense. She'd not mentioned much about it during the odd times we'd talked.

"I'd better keep looking." I was suddenly worried about her.

My parents' room had been taken over by the most elaborate poker game I'd ever seen. They'd emptied out Craig's Monopoly board to use the paper money as chips. It was all men, of course – as poker always seems to attract just-the-ladz-just-the-ladz. Predictably Will, Lottie's boyfriend, was sitting there – with a sizeable stack of orange five-hundred pound notes in front of him.

"Will," I called and he looked up, mildly annoyed

to have his concentration interrupted. Although, sometimes, really, if I'm being honest, that was just what Will's face looked like. An air of superiority, which, unfortunately, his personality didn't do much to contradict.

"All right, Amber?" He did smile, which was something. "Good party."

"Thanks. Though I really don't want anyone to have sex in the bedrooms if I can possibly help it. Have you seen Lottie?"

"Ha, I've killed two birds for you there." Will looked briefly down at his cards. "She was really drunk for some reason, so I put her to sleep in your room. Keeping the bed sex-free."

He smiled again but I scowled. "You've just left her there?" It came out more accusingly than I thought it would.

"Relax. She's in the recovery position and everything. She'll sleep it off. Probably be up again before midnight, wanting to do it all over again."

What? She was that drunk? And alone? Yes, I hadn't

checked on her until now but that's because I thought she was with Will. Why had he just left her? I mean, okay, it's annoying when your boyfriend or girlfriend gets too wasted at a party, but that doesn't mean you just leave them…does it?

"I'll go check she's okay," I said pointedly.

Will's attention was already back on the game. "Who's big blind?" he said, rather than goodbye, and I nudged the door open, biting my lip in annoyance. I walked down the landing, delighted to find that no one was copulating in Craig's bedroom either – just a bunch of band people sitting in a corner, singing along to Joel and his acoustic guitar. It was still weird to see him without Jane. I'd got so used to them coming as a pair. By the blackish circles under Joel's eyes, and the sad way in which he sang "Wonderwall", I figured he felt the same. He nodded hello and I nodded back, before turning to find Lottie.

She was fast asleep like Goldilocks, all tucked up, and looking half her age. I perched by her side, checking her vitals – breathing, okay, no sick all over my duvet, okay. Will had indeed put her in the recovery position, if I remembered it correctly from camp. She was safe, but it felt…sad to me that she'd just been left upstairs.

Lottie was not the sort of person who got left upstairs.

I spent a few minutes just looking at her, watching her sleep, all childlike and quiet and innocent. Her haircut was still a shock. Not that it didn't suit her – she was so pretty she could hack half of it off and look incredible. But it was blunt and new and she didn't ask Evie or me before getting it cut, which isn't what normally happens.

I suddenly felt desperately sad. What had happened to us? Why had we let change do this to us? I missed her so much right then. I missed her laugh. I missed her overdramatic monologues. I missed the way she always, always cared what was going on with me. I missed us… Lottie, Evie and me. All together. Always there for each other. Always honest with each other. Always.

…or so I'd thought.

And now I was going away and I hadn't even told them yet.

I wasn't sure how she was sleeping through the heavy bass shaking the floor from the room below. I couldn't stay with her though, I needed to keep an eye on the party. I'd go get Evie, put her on watch, then maybe ask Jane if she'd help too.

Will was right in that I doubted she'd be out of it for long.

Lottie was never not the life and soul of any party.

Before now anyway…

I touched her cheek, the sadness spreading through my veins like an IV drip of regret, and then stood up to get Evie.

lottie

Zzzzzzzzzzzzzzzzzzzzzzzzzzzzzz...

"CHUG CHUG CHUG CHUG CHUG CHUG CHUG."

Well, this was definitely helping get my mind off things.

I downed my drink, to a chorus of cheers. And they say peer pressure can make young people drink… I aimed at the table again, not squinting, because I've learned from many an action movie that squinting actually makes your aim worse, and threw the ping-pong ball. It bounced directly into one of Amber's cups.

Everyone erupted. I erupted. I leaped in the air in triumph. I felt very very proud of myself, and excited, and slightly tipsy, and very pleased that I could throw a ping-pong ball and, well, maybe a teeny bit more than tipsy, but good, I felt good, I felt GREAT as Amber poured her drink down her face and everyone announced me the winner and I cheered and yelled and forgot about everything and then…

…then my phone went again.

And my euphoria rose up out of me like a helium balloon and drifted through the open kitchen window.

BAD THOUGHT

Why won't he stop sending messages? It's so unfair that he won't stop sending messages.

WORSE THOUGHT

If he wasn't ill, this sort of behaviour would be considered abusive…

I shook my head, my hand itching for the phone, but also not wanting to read what it said. Knowing it would make my tummy hurt, make my heart ache, make my conscience feel conflicted.

I no longer felt tipsy or great – I just felt guilty and sad.

Amber went in search of Lottie, who we hadn't seen in ages.

Not just at the party, but at all really.

I was getting used to not having her in my life, but it wasn't something I was happy about. It felt like one of my limbs had been amputated. Lottie's checking-out had impacted my friendship with Amber too – even though we were both still here, in this town. She was angry at Lottie, I was more worried. Lottie was always the elephant in the room whenever we met up. And I couldn't believe, with everything going on with Oli, that my Spinster Club girls weren't really there. That things felt so strained I couldn't trust them enough to tell them about Oli. Not really. There was a wall where there never used to be even a line. There was a silence when there never used to be a held tongue.

I wasn't mad at just Lottie. I was mad at all of us. I was mad that we'd let this happen to us. When I needed us so much…

BAD THOUGHT

They don't need you.

I ducked out of the kitchen, holding a pint glass of water to get my mind straight. The living room was a no-go, stupid house music blasting out of it. None of us had ever listened to house music before. It must be something someone had got into at uni – another person shedding their skin, coming home only to gloat about how much they'd changed. I leaned against a wall and got out my phone. Again.

And did a smile, though it was gritted.

This one wasn't as bad as the others. All it said was:

Have a good night. I love you x x

Which would've been sweet, except he'd already sent so many messages that night. And, also, the downside of dating someone with anxiety when you have anxiety yourself is that you can see them coming a mile off.

This was a manipulative message. I would know. I'd sent many myself in the past. This was a carefully-thought-through, *look-how-innocent-it-is* message that, on the surface, you cannot complain about at all. But I knew Oli's brain. This message didn't just mean, *HaveagoodnightIloveyou.* No.

What the message also meant

Please don't forget about me on your good night.

Please reply otherwise I'll freak out.

I love you, but I hate myself and this message is coming out of that.

I am likely to have sent this while spiralling into a complete vat of despair but I've tried really hard to make this message sound really normal and natural so you won't know how much I'm spiralling right now but I'm actually quite desperate which is why I'm sending the message so please please reply, so I can feel loved, so I can know that you love me enough to see through this.

I sagged into the wall, the music making my back vibrate. I wasn't supposed to message back. His new therapist had told me as much. My own therapist had told me as much. Oli knew as much.

But who doesn't reply to a message like that?

I sighed and wrote back.

I love you too.

Which was true. It was, it really was. I loved Oli. I'd waited so long for Oli. He'd waited so long for me. He was the purest soul I'd ever met. So much so that he made me use phrases like "purest soul". And yet... and yet...

BAD THOUGHT

He is ruining your life right now.

BAD THOUGHT

And you worked so hard for this life, Evie.
You worked *so* hard for this life.

My phone went again and I felt like screaming.

Sorry, I know I'm not supposed to message you so much x

I'd held my phone up, ready to chuck it against the wall in frustration when I heard...

"Evie?"

"Jane?"

"Hello, stranger." She started walking down the stairs, nudging people out the way. We hugged when she reached the bottom – one of those floppy, awkward hugs when you both tap out straight away.

"Jane!" I yelled to be heard over the bass. "How are you? You look so different!"

"Ha, do I?" She sounded delighted with the comment, like it was a compliment. I hardly recognized her. Gone was her pink hair. Gone were all her Joel-acquired piercings. Gone were her eyeliner and black nail polish. Gone were her band T-shirts. Instead she wore dark blue skinny jeans with wedge heels and this see-through but smart white blouse. She had just a hint of red lipstick on and a high ponytail, framed with wisps of hair and a big hairband. She looked about twenty-five.

"You really do. What happened?"

"Oh, nothing. I just grew up, I think. I'm having the most amazing time in Bristol, Evie. It's soooo incredible there."

Why was Jane talking like that? Her accent was all off, slightly more rah.

"And did I tell you I've got a new boyfriend? His name's Harry and he's super smart, Evie. He's really into politics, he wants to be an MP."

"He'll have to fight Lottie off then." I smiled the weird smile I always found myself wearing when I spoke to Jane, like I was an audience member and she was the show. If Jane was in a show, it would've been called *The Chameleon* because of how often she morphed personalities based on who had the most social collateral.

Jane's face screwed up. "Does Lottie still think she can do that?"

"What's that supposed to mean?"

"Woah, I didn't mean it in a bad way, I was just asking. I mean, what happened last year, with the papers, and Teddy, you'd think it would've put her off. That's all. I was telling Harry about that actually, and he said you've got to be careful with that sort of thing in a life of politics. Even though what Teddy did was totally, totally wrong, that story will come out if Lottie gets into politics seriously."

"She *is* into politics seriously," I interrupted. "She's working for the WEP alongside her Philosophy, Politics and Economics degree, and has her own column in the UCL newspaper." I could almost feel my eyes turn red with rage.

I realized then – I'd had it with Jane. I'd had it with people who ask how you are but only because you'll ask how they are in return and then they'll talk so much you may as well be a mirror instead of a person. She'd broken Joel's heart when she'd dumped him. Over the phone, not even in person. They'd gone out for over two years and she'd just – *whoosh* – vanished to Bristol and told him it was over within two weeks. Oli and I had had to take him to the pub many times – I'd even seen him cry. We'd only just stopped him cutting off his prized ponytail "In tribute to her" one night when he was wasted.

"Oh," Jane said. "Well, that's cool for her, I guess."

"Yep."

There was an awkward silence while I waited for her to ask me how I was. Not that I would answer honestly of course, but still, just to be asked would be nice. But all Jane said was, "I can't believe this year is ending, so much has happened, hasn't it?"

And, even through my anger, I found myself nodding.

So much had happened.

New Year's Eve was so weird. It was like birthdays in that it forced you to confront what you'd done with your silly little life and compare it to what you should've done. *Was it enough? Did I do enough? Did I live enough?*

It was bullshit. Because you never live enough. Not when it's so easy to sabotage the opportunities of life.

It made you think back to previous New Year's Eves...

Last year, Lottie's project had just finished and we'd all been triumphant and excitable for weeks. Anna had another of her legendary house parties, inviting the whole college, and even put up a marquee in her garden. We'd drunk and laughed and cheered and hugged. When the countdown started, Oli pulled me around the corner of the house, his cheeks red with alcohol, his eyes piercingly happy, and he'd said "I love you" for the first time ever, just before midnight. It was happiness that I'd never felt before – the sort where you're quite sure you could hoverboard or fly or whatever. We'd been kissing like the crazy people that we were when the others all crept up on us, jumping on Oli's back, pulling us into a group hug.

So much has happened in a year.

Now Oli doesn't smile. Oli doesn't drink. Oli doesn't even leave his own house, let alone pull me around the corners of other ones.

Lottie isn't here.

Amber is here but only in person – her brain has seemed checked out for a while now.

Happy New Year, I guess.

And, just as I was about to make an excuse to Jane so I could go cry somewhere, I heard Amber.

"Evie?" she called down the stairs. "I need your help."

11 O'CLOCK

Evie was chatting to Jane at the bottom of the stairs, getting pretty pissed off by the looks of it. I wasn't surprised. Their entire friendship existed only as long as Evie ignored the fact Jane was a self-obsessed A-to-the-Hole.

I called down, and the look of relief on Evie's face suggested she was finally catching on to the whole *Jane-is-a-twat* factor.

"What is it?" Her voice hardly audible over the music.

"It's Lottie, she's passed out. Can you…?"

The most horrendous crash echoed throughout the house, followed by applause and everyone cheering.

"Oh God! What the hell was that?"

I ran downstairs, following the clapping noise. Evie fell into step with me as I dashed down the hallway, into the kitchen, where…where…

…the entire beer pong table was upside down.

Kyle stood there, with his arms up in the air, like he was frozen in time.

He found my face. "It was an accident!"

I blinked. I blinked again. There was liquid all over the kitchen floor. Beer liquid. Sticky beer liquid. Sylvia was holding a roll of kitchen towel and, when she saw me, she just dropped the whole thing onto the kitchen floor without unravelling it and it exploded into total drenched-ness, like a used tampon – doubling in size almost instantly.

"Kyle." My voice was quiet, but it cut through the party's air like a knife through something really easy to cut.

"I'm sorry, I'm sorry, I got carried away." His voice was quite slurred and I tilted my head, smiling at him a little. Britain's binge-drinking culture was rubbing off on him. It made him ten million times more adorable, but my kitchen was still wrecked.

"Right, everyone, help me clean up."

People kicked into action well enough. I dug out more kitchen roll from under the sink, and handed it out. "Rip some off, and THEN mop the floor," I instructed, looking pointedly at Sylvia.

Some of the boys put the table the right way up again, others moved bits of paper around the floor using their feet.

"Umm, Amber?" Evie asked. "I'm sorry your kitchen is destroyed and all, but is it okay if I just watch the clean-up?"

I nodded. "That's fine. Actually, while I'm busy with this, do you mind going and checking on Lottie? She's asleep in my room, but Will just left her there." I ripped off a bin liner and collected up some discarded cups.

"He just left her, like, unconscious?"

I raised an eyebrow. "I know. He's playing poker upstairs. I think…"

Someone asked me for more kitchen roll and I got

distracted by the clean-up. I was just crouching on the balls of my feet, soaking up the last of it, when I heard the thud of the kitchen door being flung back on its hinges.

"CAREFUL!" I yelled. "I don't want my dad to gut me..." I stood up to see who was breaking my house, and there Lottie stood, her hair all on end, her face red.

"Lottie, you're up. I—"

"You're LEAVING?" she yelled, just as Evie appeared in a fluster behind her. "You're FUCKING LEAVING?"

lottie

Sleeeeeeeeeeeeep.

Lovely sleeeepppppp.

Zzzzzzz…

Oufft.

A giant weight fell onto me, crushing my legs.

"OUCH."

"Sorry, we didn't know anyone was in here."

I opened my eyes in the dimness to see Ethan and some girl, still half-sitting on me.

"Get off me!" I demanded, my legs feeling like they were turning cartoon-flat. "Jeez!"

Ethan and the random girl laughed and got up. The strap of her top was around her shoulder, and her skirt was all hitched up around her waist. She didn't even seem that embarrassed as she pulled it down.

"What are you doing in bed anyway?" Ethan asked, readjusting his jumper, which was up around his armpits – probably about to be pulled off, until they fell on top of me.

"I've had a very hard day, I'm just having a rest..." I stumbled, feeling quite out of it. Where was I again? Oh yeah. Amber's party. What was it again? Oh yes, New Year's Eve. My mouth felt very dry... Oh yeah, I'd been drinking. Quite a bit.

Had I fallen asleep?

And, hang on, Will...I saw Will! He put me to bed. Where the heck was he?

Ethan and the random stumbled back towards the door – the music got louder and then quieter again as they pushed each other out onto the landing.

"Let's try another room," I heard Ethan say. I probably should've tried to stop them but I wanted to finish this lovely nap. I closed my eyes again…

But I couldn't sleep. Will. He'd just left me here? Alone? He hadn't sat by my bedside and stroked my hair and whispered that he loved me as I slept it off? Or, at the very least, thought *Fuck you, Lottie, you've got wankered and now you've ruined my evening* on the inside, but on the outside still sat and looked after me? That's what you DO in a couple. God. There was that first weekend visit to Royal Holloway when he'd decided to try a space cake and spent the entire evening vomiting in the bathroom. I'd had to meet most of his housemates over the top of his head down the loo, but I'd STAYED with him all night. Even though my eyeliner had been totally on point that evening, and everyone knows you shouldn't let perfectly-applied cat flicks go to waste.

I huddled my legs up to my chest, falling over onto my side, trying not to cry. Why was everything going wrong? I took out my phone to check the time. Jeez – it was less than an hour to midnight. Was Will just going to leave me unconscious when the bell struck twelve? I didn't know what bell it was really, but I knew people who loved each other tended to like to be around each other when the random bell did whatever it does. I took a selfie to see how gross I looked, and the flash of the flash made me see stars.

When the stars had stopped, there was a pretty disastrous face staring out of my phone.

"Uh God," I whispered. "Will, I now understand why you didn't want to stroke this hair."

I sat up, my head swooshing. I needed make-up. Stat. I would make myself look incredible and find Will and apologize for being a drunken mess and not bring up the other week, and the clock would strike twelve and the bell would toll and we'd kiss like we were in the movies and everything would be okay again. New year, new start. Maybe my New Year's resolution could be to try harder with my housemates? Or stop lying to everyone about how happy I was?

Was I doing that?

Maybe.

Oooh, I bet Amber's amazing light-reflecting moisturizer was in here somewhere. The really posh one you can only get in America. She never lets me borrow it, but, right now, if I could ask her, she'd definitely say yes, if she could see the state of my face.

I rolled onto the floor and got up from all fours. Then made my way over to her dressing table where she keeps all her junk.

God, Amber was a slob! There was crap EVERYWHERE. Where was that bottle? It was yellow, I thought. Oooh, perfume. I picked it up and sprayed some on. Before remembering I already had perfume on. Hmm. I looked at the bottle. It had *hints of vanilla*, and my perfume was citrus. Citrus and vanilla sort of went, didn't they? I knocked a few things over – "Whoops" – and bent down to pick them up, hoping I'd not smashed anything.

A stupid little bottle had rolled under the bed. I sighed and got down clumsily to reach for it, praying I didn't discover one of Amber's infamous plates of mouldy sandwich.

Where was the bottle? What was my hand touching? Hang on, there was all this paper in the way. I grabbed it and pulled it out. That was better. I reached back under and my fingers grasped the cool glass of the pot. Got it! I was just withdrawing my hand triumphantly, when I glanced down at the stack of papers and saw…

We are delighted to confirm your place at Rhode Island School of Design. Attached is all the course information, as well as the forms we need you to fill in regarding college accommodation. As an international student, we invite you to start two weeks before term begins to take part in our "cultural introduction" program, where you can meet other international students and orientate yourself…

What?

I put the letter down. Picked it back up again.

WHAT?

Amber?

Rhode Island?

Rhode Island isn't in England. It's in America.

CONFIRM YOUR PLACE?

This wasn't just an offer. This was a confirmation.

Amber had a *confirmed* place at a university in America?

Amber was leaving?

Leaving us?

Tears sprang to my eyes instantly, my throat feeling coarse and hollow. My stomach felt so sick, so quickly, that I had to sit down on the floor and clutch at it.

She can't go. It's so far! We need her. It's *us*. Why is she going? Is it to be with Kyle? It must be. WHAT SORT OF SHIT FEMINIST IS SHE?

She can't go.

She can't.

What am I going to do?

What is EVIE going to do? I mean, she's the one with OCD, and Amber thinks it's okay just to leave the country? When Evie can't fly?

The shock and horror was quickly replaced by something else... Anger.

Not anger – rage.

My fists curled in, my hands shook. She can't go,

it's so selfish, *why why why why?* Blood flung itself around my body.

Then I had a new thought.

She was leaving and she hadn't even bothered to tell us?

We were her BEST FRIENDS and she'd not told us? Not even discussed it with us? Not talked it through? Seen what we thought? Seen if we MIND?

I stood up. Amber couldn't just leave. She couldn't just not tell us! What was she thinking? Where was she?

evie

Lottie was still drunk, but that didn't stop her blowing my world into chunks. Bleedy, oozing chunks of horror.

"You're fucking leaving?" she yelled in Amber's face, with such force I imagined Amber's hair being blown back.

Leaving? LEAVING?

No no no no no no no no no no no no.

But Amber's face, oh God, it told me everything I didn't want to know. She went red, her eyes filling with tears. I saw her blink them away.

"How...how?"

"How did I find out?" Lottie yelled, waving her arms around like a maniac. "I found your confirmation letter. In your room. Where you'd all abandoned me apparently."

"We were just coming to get you."

"Don't change the subject," Lottie snapped. "What's going on? You're leaving?"

There was quietness between us against the loud chaos of the surrounding party as Amber gulped, then said, "I'm leaving, yes. I got a place at Rhode Island School of Design. In America."

BAD THOUGHT

Nononononononononononononononononononono

BAD THOUGHT

She can't. She's all I have. She can't, she can't.

My body took over; it grabbed the steering wheel off me and twisted it until I was skidding and screeching in the direction of *total and complete panic.*

"Amber?" I managed to stammer.

She'd crossed her arms all defensively, her prickles up.

"And when were you planning on telling us?" Lottie demanded, her pupils all over the place. Still wasted, though the anger seemed genuine. It was carving through her intoxication, sobering her up enough to say lots of things she actually meant rather than drunk-meant. "Were you going to bother telling us at all?"

"Of course—"

But Lottie cut her off. "Or were you just going to leave a note? *Hi, girls. Just to let you know I've FUCKING EMIGRATED, tootles for now. Laters.*" Lottie's arms were whirling all over the place, like she was a drunk windmill. People in the kitchen started to stare. "Or were you just going to send a postcard, with *Guess what?* written on the back?"

"Oh, you can talk, Lottie!" Amber's voice trebled in

volume, matching Lottie's now. "You've only gone to London, it's practically DOWN THE ROAD, and yet we never hear from you, do we, Evie?"

It wasn't a question I was supposed to answer.

BAD THOUGHT

Amber can't leave.

BAD THOUGHT

Everyone is leaving.

BAD THOUGHT

I'm being left behind because I'm boring and broken and too scared to go away anywhere, and they'll forget me and I'll be alone for ever.

Good thought

You won't be alone though, Evie. You've got Oli...

BAD THOUGHT

You'll be stuck with Oli, with no one to talk to about it.

WORSE THOUGHT

You can't talk to your friends about it anyway.

Amber was still yelling, on the defensive. Her default setting. "So don't you have a go at me, Lottie. What excuse do you have? For never coming home? For never inviting us there?"

Lottie's mouth fell open. "What? What the hell? I see you guys all the time."

Amber laughed bitterly. "No you don't! You're only with us this Christmas because all your London friends aren't here. Don't pretend that's not true."

Lottie's mouth was still open. She closed it. Opened it again. "That's not true," she whispered, so quietly I could hardly hear it.

It was just then that Kyle arrived – back from taking the bin bags out. He scooped his arm around Amber and asked, "Hey, whatsup?"

amber

I wasn't handling it well.

The part of me that wasn't TOTALLY ANGRY could see that. But that part was hiding in the corner, uninterested in taking part in this conversation.

I say conversation – it was a fight.

How did Lottie find out? That girl – that bloody girl! I swear she's the most irritating, know-it-all, smug, interfering… Oh God, I didn't want it to come out like this. Evie's face! She looked like everything was falling apart. And I guess for her, it was. But I didn't have time to process that, because Lottie was still drunk and yelling in my face.

Kyle's arms curled around me, squeezing me, asking what was up.

"I'll tell you whatsup," Lottie said. God, her voice was hateful. What had happened to her? Why was she being like this? "Your girlfriend is apparently leaving her entire life behind to be with a boy. Some feminist!"

Okay – now it really was a fight.

"Woah!" Kyle held up his arm, casting a protective spell around me. "Lottie, calm down."

Uh oh. He'd told Lottie to calm down.

She ignited.

"DON'T YOU DARE TELL ME TO CALM DOWN, I'M ALLOWED TO NOT CALM DOWN, FUCKING PATRIARCHY ALWAYS TELLING ME TO CALM DOWN..."

While I yelled over her, "How DARE you make this about feminism! Do you not think I'm capable of making a decision for me? What sort of friend are you? Aren't we supposed to support each other's choices? I mean, HOW DARE YOU?"

And Kyle kept going, "Woah woah woah, I didn't mean it like that. Both of you, come on, let's take some time. Let's go outside...breathe, breathe... Evie? Are you okay?" Evie was flat-out crying, and part of me felt so sorry for her, but the other angry part of me was just SO ANGRY and sad and pissed off because I was scared to leave, and I needed their support and I couldn't believe I was leaving them, because I loved them, but I HATED LOTTIE and, and...

Bloody Will crashed through the kitchen door, holding a bottle of beer. He saw the state of everything and said, "What the hell is going on?"

Why was Amber yelling at me?

She was the one LEAVING, she was the one who HADN'T EVEN TOLD US.

And now she's spouting all this crap about me going off to London?

I mean, what?

This was going all wrong, and my mouth was SO dry, and, what?!

What does she mean I've just buggered off to London? That I don't invite them? Has it occurred to them I'm TOO EMBARRASSED to invite them to London?

To show them just how much my housemates hate me. And how alone I feel, even with the column and the WEP and all the good stuff – that none of it counts, because nobody seems to like me that much?

I was so angry. I was angry at Amber for leaving. And I was angry at tonight for going so wrong. And I was angry at Will for not having sex with me and then leaving me alone in the dark. And I was angry at the world and the future and growing up and becoming an adult and all the other things that just do not turn out how they're supposed to.

And then Kyle is here, telling me to CALM DOWN?

I can't really remember what I said. Just yelling, and flailing, and Evie was crying and I felt TERRIBLE. Because Amber was leaving.

She can't leave.

What are we going to do without her?

HER BIG ANGRY FACE THAT I HATE?

I know, I'll keep yelling at her and Kyle, and insulting them until they agree to change their minds. Perfect plan – perfect!

And then Will was there.

Will. Swearing, and clutching a beer.

"Will!" I yelled, and I put my arms down instantly. I didn't want him to see I'd started a fight. I didn't want him to see I was out of control. I'm not sure why. I mean, one of the reasons I loved Will was that he'd fallen in love with me for me – for angry, complicated, over-dramatic me.

Well, I thought he had.

Recently it's seemed like it's actually all those bits of me he silently wishes away.

"Lottie, what's going on?"

"Nothing to see here!" I said brightly, trying to stand in front of Amber and Kyle and a crying Evie.

"Oh, that's just great," Amber shouted from behind me. "Turn your back on this. Just scream in my face and then turn your back on this."

Shh, Amber! I thought. *Not now! Not when I need to impress Will!*

"Lottie?" Will peered around my body to analyse the scene. "Seriously, what's going on?" He didn't sound interested, only annoyed. Oh God, I was annoying him. I couldn't annoy him. Why am I always annoying people?

"Amber's moving to America." It was the first time Evie had spoken and her voice, her voice almost sobered me up. It was so sad, so quiet, so restrained. As usual, Evie wasn't yelling or screaming or telling everyone off. She was always so much better – the peacekeeper, the chill one, even with everything.

"Oh." Will pushed his glasses up his nose. "Right."

"To be with her boyfriend," I couldn't help adding, in a high-pitched bitchy voice, glaring at Kyle.

"Stop it!" Amber screamed. "Have you even thought to ask me why I'm going? Because then I might actually tell you. Have you ever thought how hard it was for me to make this decision?"

Shit – the decision was made. She really was leaving…

"I couldn't, could I?" I replied, not yelling because Will was watching and looking slightly bored…or maybe I was imagining it. "Because you DIDN'T TELL US."

"I was going to."

"When?"

"Well, it's hard because you're always so terribly busy in London." She used the same bitchy voice as me.

I shook my head. I didn't know what to think or feel. Everything was blurring. And on top of that, Will just turned and walked away. Walked away! I needed to sort things with him. I turned and followed him into the rest of the party.

"Lottie, don't go," Evie said. "It's almost midnight!"

But I ignored her, and pushed through a group of people blocking my way. Trying to get to him.

We were left there, without her.

Amber laughed, quickly, sharply. "I can't believe her. She just walks off, in the middle of an argument, to follow her boyfriend. And she tries to call ME a bad feminist?"

She turned to smile at me, to see if I would nod and agree.

But I was spiralling…

BAD THOUGHT

You have no one.

BAD THOUGHT

You're the crazy one, being left behind.
The crazy ones always get left behind.

I couldn't imagine life without Amber, life without the three of us. Yes, uni was okay, and the people I'd met were great, but they weren't my Spinster Club. Lottie going to London was one thing… It was new, I sort of didn't blame her for getting caught up in it. I knew she'd come back.

But Amber… America.

BAD THOUGHT

You can't fly to America, Evie. Think of all the recycled air in planes.

"Evie?" Amber's face softened, her eyes wide, wet with the hint of tears. Kyle's arms were around her, kissing the top of her head, soothing her.

I didn't have anyone to soothe me.

Not any more.

I shook my head. "I can't believe you didn't say anything," was all I could say. Because if I said much more, I would shatter into so many pieces I'd turn into dust.

"Evie, I was going to! I just wanted to...I was just waiting for..."

"You're actually going?"

Maybe she'd shake her head. Maybe she'd say she hadn't decided yet. Maybe she'd say "only for a year". Maybe this was a joke. Maybe this was a phase. Maybe maybe...

"I'm going, Evie. Please...if you'd just hear me out..."

But I'd stopped listening. I didn't want to hear it. I couldn't hear it. I couldn't pretend to be happy for her, not when I was so sad for me. Sad for me – lost, silly me. Who couldn't leave their hometown, who couldn't get on planes, who couldn't have adventures, who had a boyfriend who couldn't even leave the house. My stupid tiny life which will always be stupid and tiny because my brain won't let it be anything but. I thought I was doing okay. I thought I was getting there. But all I was doing was getting left behind.

"It's almost midnight," I said. "I have to call Oli."

"Evie? Evie!"

But I grabbed my coat from the bannisters and pushed myself out into the back garden to call my boyfriend.

My crazy, lonely boyfriend.

Who was all I seemed to have left.

MIDNIGHT

amber

People were yelling, things were smashing, the party was getting out of hand.

"Everyone into the living room for the countdown," someone shouted, like it was their house.

I was running upstairs to my bedroom, Kyle chasing after me.

I was crying.

"Amber? Amber!" he called after me, worry bleeding through his voice.

I pushed through my bedroom door and flopped head first onto the bed, crying directly into my pillow, which smelled slightly of Lottie and her sick.

It was too much. Them knowing. It made it real. And they were both so angry. I couldn't blame them. Well, I could blame Lottie. It was so like her to make it all drama and yelling and about her.

I felt the pressure of Kyle perching on the end of the bed.

"Amber?" he asked, stroking my foot.

I cried in reply.

"Amber, it will be okay. It's just Lottie letting off steam is all."

Letting off steam? I smiled into the pillow. Only Kyle would use the phrase "letting off steam". I sat myself up.

"Did you see Evie's face? She hates me."

"She's just surprised. It wasn't right for Lottie to confront you like that."

I looked down at the carpet, where my papers were. Where she'd made the discovery…

"I can't believe I'm leaving them behind."

He pulled me closer and started rubbing my back, kissing my head. Always there for me.

"You're not leaving them anywhere. You'll still be in touch all the time, they can come visit…"

"Evie won't be able to." My hand went to my mouth the moment I had the thought. She wouldn't, she'd not been on a plane for years.

"She can build up to it. And you'll come back and visit all the time. It will be fine," Kyle said. "And—"

We were interrupted by yelling from downstairs.

"TEN

NINE

EIGHT."

"It's midnight," I said, even though it was obvious. Kyle stood to go downstairs but I pulled him back down. I didn't want to see in this new year with anyone around me. This year was going to change everything. It was going to be a year I marked in my life as the one when everything shifted. This time next year, I'd probably be in the States. It wouldn't even be midnight yet. And everyone would have American accents and…oh God… what was I doing?

"FIVE

FOUR

THREE..."

But Kyle. His arms around me, his lips pressed into my forehead, the way I just felt so...full. So safe. So me. I had to be with him. I had to leave. It broke my heart. But I had to. I had to give my life a shot. I had to go where the love was...

"TWO..."

I looked up at him. "I love you," I told him, and his smile stretched so far across his face I'm surprised it didn't break.

"I love you too. It's going to be okay, Amber, you're going to be okay."

"HAPPY NEW YEAR!!!!!!!!!!!"

The cheers bounced up the stairs, the hoots of horns, the pop of party poppers. I felt that weird mix of drama and anticlimax that you always feel on the first breath of a new year. I hugged Kyle tight and he gently swayed me as a rowdy nonsensical version of "Auld Lang Syne" thundered up through the floor.

"SHOULD AULD ACQUAINTANCE BE FORGOT AND NEVER BROUGHT TO MIIIIIIND..."

Oh God, would Lottie and Evie become old acquaintances? Would they merge into the past? Would their outlines disappear? Would we not be able to keep it up?

Or worse, would I develop an American twang?

"Everything's going to change," I mumbled into Kyle's hard shoulder.

"That's just what life is."

"But I don't want things to change."

"Don't you?"

And I thought about living in this house, always feeling like a stranger. And I thought about how...good America had been for me. How it had flaked off my cynicism, unravelled my armour, made me smile and realize good things can happen, and that I am a good thing.

But I also thought of the girls, and weekly emails becoming monthly, and monthly emails becoming *Sorry it took me so long to reply,* until we didn't really reply any more at all.

"I don't want things to change with my friends."

Kyle released me from the hug, and held me at arm's length. He put on his crap British accent and said: "Well, bloody find them and tell them that then."

"Will! Will? Wait up."

For a moment I didn't think he'd stop for me. But he paused in the hallway, and I caught up.

"Hey, Lottie. You all right?" He looked everywhere but in my eyes, mostly at the top of my head. I mean, my hair was a mess, but he'd seen it like this more often than not. "What was going on back there?"

"I told you. Amber's moving to America." I snorted. "To be with Kyle. Anyway" – I reached out, putting my arm around him, craving touch – "I should be yelling at you, not her. Why did you leave me all alone in her room?" I laughed, to show I didn't mind. When I really did mind, quite a lot.

Will didn't smile, instead he looked quite pained. Oh God, something was wrong. I could feel it in my loins, and my loins are never wrong. "I was only gone a moment, you were out cold."

"You would've missed kissing me at midnight?" I smiled seductively, as much as you can with your mouth closed as you probably smell like vomit.

Again, Will didn't smile. Well, he did. But it was all closed-lips and squinty eyes and for show and I couldn't pretend something wasn't up. I wasn't Amber.

So, just as he said, "Shall we go into the living room? It's almost the countdown," I said, "Will, what the hell is going on?"

He scratched his head. "What do you mean?"

"You're being all weird."

"No I'm not."

"You are. You've hardly spoken to me since you got here."

"You're just drunk, Lottie."

"Don't gaslight me! I know you. I know when you're being weird. And you know me. You know I'm not going to stop bugging you until you tell me. So why don't you save yourself an unpleasant battering and just talk already?"

I was holding myself up using the wall, leaning into it. But my voice didn't sound as drunk as I felt, and Will must've heard it. Because he sighed a big, heavy sigh and then said words that sent dread catapulting around my bodily parts.

"Argh, I didn't want to do this tonight... Can we go somewhere?"

I gulped, which is quite an achievement when your mouth is as dry as the inside of a vacuum cleaner. "Let's go outside."

And, to pretend I had some control of the situation, I walked past him and pushed through the front door.

It was so cold outside, my breath frosting and drifting off. I wanted to hug my arms to myself, but felt like I needed to look brave. Which was a worry. I turned on my heel, the second I'd stepped off the front step and said, "So, what is it then?"

Though I knew, I think I knew...and I couldn't...

Will kept scratching his head, pulling his hair up on end. His eyes behind the thick frames of his glasses still looked everywhere but at me.

"It's just...I'm just...I told you, I didn't want to do this tonight."

"If you're going to break up with me, I'd rather you didn't hold onto that information." It came out sharp, bitter. Will's mouth dropped open, but he didn't deny it. He didn't deny it straight away. And if you're not about to break up with someone, you would deny it straight away.

"Oh God," I said, tears springing to my eyes, but I wouldn't let them spill. No, do not let him see you cry. But Will saw through it, softening, stepping forward to hold my face in his hands.

"Oh, Lottie, it's okay."

I shook my head to get rid of him. "No, don't touch me. Explain. Tell me why you're ending this."

"I'm not ending this."

He wasn't? He reached out, took my hand, squeezed it.

He looked so pained and I melted a little, even with the air this cold. Maybe it was fine. Maybe he just had a disease or something – we could deal with that. A non-terminal one, like mono. I'm not sure what mono is, but I think it's safeish.

"So, what's going on?" I looked up to meet his gaze. "You've been so weird."

"But you have too."

"What?"

"I don't *want* to break up with you," he said...making my heart lift a little.

Shouting came from inside.

"TEN

NINE

EIGHT..."

The countdown had begun, but I hardly noticed it, hanging on his every word. Wanting so much for this to be okay. So something in my life was okay. Yes, we'd been weird for a while now, but at least I could tell myself that I had this part of my life sorted, the romance box well and truly ticked with lovely, sexy film-maker Will.

"But, when I was away skiing, I was thinking, well… do you not think…"

"SEVEN

SIX

FIVE…"

"…we're a bit too…young…"

"FOUR

THREE…"

"…to be in a relationship this serious? I mean, what I'm trying to say is…"

"TWO

ONE…"

"…that we should take a break from each other."

"HAPPY NEW YEAR!!!!!!!"

Cheers erupted around us, echoing from all the houses, shooting into my heart as it cracked open and spilled out onto the manicured lawn of Amber's front garden.

"Will, you just broke up with me."

He shook his head. "No, I didn't. I just think we need to talk."

"About breaking up?"

"No...well...about having a break."

"That's the same thing, Will." My voice tried to break on the word "Will" but I pulled it back, crossing my arms further. *Don't let him see you upset, don't let him see you upset.*

"It's just, Lottie... Look, I love you, you know I love you..." *Don't cry don't cry don't cry.* "But come on. We're both only nineteen. We're at different unis. I don't think we should be tied down. Don't you think maybe we should be...well...free?"

"You want to fuck other people?"

"No! It's not like that. It's not like that at all."

"I can't believe you've just dumped me, at midnight, on New Year's Eve, so you can shove your penis into other people."

Will pulled a face. "Don't be crass."

"I can be however I want, you're breaking up with me so you can get laid."

"I'm not, I'm not..." He sighed and, to be fair, he looked sort of broken. But it was him doing the breaking

– of himself, of me, of us. "Come on, Lottie. Us, you and me. We're not the sort of people who get tied into a relationship when we're this young. I love you…"

Then don't break up with me.

"…but I don't know, I'm finding it hard us doing long distance…"

"It's less than an hour's journey!"

He ignored me. "And there was this girl I met, skiing…" He saw my face. "I didn't do anything but, well, I wanted to. And I'm sure you want to too. I don't want to resent you, and I don't want you to resent me. I can see you resent me…like when I last came to visit…"

I dropped my mouth open. "You were sucking up to Heather and everyone, you acted like you hated me all weekend!"

"You were being weird all weekend, Lottie! You, like, didn't want to leave your room. And I was just being friendly. I'm a film-maker, I get to know people. I thought you liked that about me, but you acted like I was a deserter or something."

I shook my head, trying to dislodge whatever new

reality this was that was settling into my life like unwelcome snow. No Amber, no Will. What was going on? Will was still talking – it was never like him to talk more than me, but he was rambling, like my stunned silence was making him nervous.

"Look, I've never met a girl like you. I adore you. And maybe we can get back together when we're older? I just don't want us to sour. I care about us too much to sour."

"So you're breaking up with me to save us?"

It was his turn to shake his head. "Stop trying to score points, I'm trying to have a serious conversation. I'm trying to be honest... Lottie...I love you..." His voice broke then, and he looked up, meeting my eye.

"Don't say you love me if you're breaking up with me, Will. Those two things can't co-exist."

Will was crying, his face had gone red and blotchy, his glasses weren't sitting quite right and all my insides threw themselves at each other, in confusion, in pain, in longing, in hurt. "I've never loved anyone before. I don't know what to do...I...I..." He was proper crying, pushing his glasses askew as he tried to stuff the tears back into his eyes. I kept shaking my head, not sure what to do. Will was crying. The boy I loved was crying. But, well, he was crying because of something HE was doing, not me. What are you supposed to do about that? I reached out slowly, touching his arm. It was as cold as my fingers. He grabbed my hand with his other hand and sort of pulled me into him, until I was flat against his chest.

"I don't understand why you're doing this," I managed to say, as my own tears spilled.

"I think you do, Lottie. I just think you're too scared to let go of us right now. I know you're finding things hard at uni. But that's not a reason to hold onto something that's not right. I know you know that. I know you're going to thank me for doing this, in time. Sorry, the timing is shit…I thought I could avoid doing this tonight. I'm…I'm so sorry, Lottie."

He leaned his forehead against mine, pulled me in for a kiss and I kissed him back blearily, our tears merging. How had this evening come to this? How had life gone this way? How can any good come from a year that starts with your first love kissing you on the forehead, whispering "Goodbye" and walking away from you, leaving you sinking into the lawn, your heartbreak bleeding out onto the cold frost of the ground?

He answered on the first ring.

"Evie? What is it? Is everything okay?"

Only a person with anxiety would know straight away if an anxious person was calling in a state of anxiety.

I was already crying. "No."

"What is it? What's happened?"

The shock and grief overtook me and I was unable to talk for a good minute as I sank back into the wall, sobs erupting from my guts, coughing them up like phlegm. I almost couldn't breathe.

Oli yelled down the phone with worry. "Evie? Evie?!

What is it? Are you okay? Has someone done something to you? Evie? Please talk to me, EVIE!"

Eventually I managed to say, "I'm fine, I'm safe. It's just…just…" And the cries won again and I sank so far back into the wall that the pebbled stucco grazed my back through my top.

Oli seemed to calm a little, though he kept saying, "What's wrong? What's wrong?"

BAD THOUGHT

He should be here for this, not on the other end of a phone.

And I cried harder with guilt for even thinking that. I slid to the ground, huddling my knees up, just crying and crying into my mobile.

BAD THOUGHT

Why not touch that rock over there seven times? See if that will stop Amber from leaving?

And the urge, the urge was so strong. Even though it was silly and stupid and wouldn't work and would be selfish if it did work.

"Evie, you're scaring me."

"Amber's moving to America," I said finally. "Lottie just found her confirmation letter from an American uni upstairs."

There was a silence as Oli digested. Then, "Oh, Evie. That's such a shock. Are you okay?"

I shook my head into the phone. "I can't believe she's leaving!" I couldn't breathe, I couldn't get the air in. I was trying, but the air wouldn't come. I coughed and gulped.

"Don't try to believe it right now," Oli said. "You just need to get used to the shock. Are you breathing properly? In for five, out for seven. Look, I'll do it for you." He started taking deep long breaths down the phone, over-exaggerated and slow.

Shouting came from inside.

"TEN

NINE

EIGHT…"

"Oli, it's almost midnight!" I managed to gasp down the line.

"I don't care. Come on, breathe with me. In for five, out for seven."

My throat was sore and constricted but I tried to match my breathing to his. His voice was so calm, so sure, I felt almost entranced by it.

"SEVEN

SIX

FIVE

FOUR…"

"In for five, out for seven," he repeated.

My heart rate started to calm down, my hands stopped shaking so hard.

"THREE

TWO…"

"In for five, out for seven. Good girl, Evie."

"HAPPY NEW YEAR."

And we saw in the year together on a fresh exhale of breath.

A NEW YEAR

I needed to find the others.

Kyle and I went downstairs, walking into the euphoria of a new year. Loads of people were still doing that cross-your-arms-and-hold-hands-with-a-stranger thing and belting out a slurry version of "Auld Lang Syne". Again. Even though it was obvious no one in my house knew the second line. People kept grabbing us, hugging us, holding our arms up in celebration – the contents of emptied party poppers strewn over everyone's heads. Then Joel put on "Jump Around" and the entire downstairs leaped into the air, dragging Kyle and me into headlocks. I tried looking for the girls but couldn't see them anywhere.

Kyle managed to break us free, and we quickly checked the rest of the house – finding only Ethan, naked, with some random girl in my little brother's bedroom. "Ethan!"

"Sorry." He smiled as we closed the door.

He obviously wasn't sorry, and I didn't really mind. It was only Craig's room. Maybe I wouldn't even wash the sheets.

"That's disgusting, Amber," Kyle said, and I put my hand to my mouth.

"Whoops. Didn't realize I'd said that out loud."

"They're not here," he said. "Do you want me to hold the fort so you can go look for them?"

It was moments like this. Moments when he knew exactly what to say that made me sure I wasn't a total idiot for removing the ocean between us.

"Would you mind?"

"Not at all. Go get them. Sort it out. The night's not over yet."

I fled downstairs, out the back door, into the freezing air.

And I found Evie.

She was sitting with her back against the wall, talking quietly into her phone. Tears on her cheeks. She sensed me looming, and looked up, held up her hand to say give her a moment.

She wasn't giving me the finger. That was a good sign.

"Amber's here… I know…thank you. I love you…" She hung up.

"Evie? Are you okay?"

She rubbed under her eyes and stared up at me. "You're really leaving, aren't you?" she asked quietly.

My own eyes stung. "I'm sorry. I was going to tell you. I just…I don't know."

She let out a smile. "You deserve to be happy, Amber."

My eyes stung so much they leaked a little. "But I'll miss you."

She shook her head. "Don't. You'll set me off again."

I crouched down, so we were almost eye level, balancing on the balls of my feet. "Are you okay?"

Evie shook her head. "No. Yes. I want to be a good friend and feel happy for you…"

"But?"

"But I don't want you to go." She started crying, and I started crying. I tipped over onto her, and we cried together into each other's shoulders, making them wet.

"It's so freezing," Evie said, between tears, "that I might literally give you a cold shoulder."

I laughed, then the laughing made me cry harder.

"Oh God, what a pair we make," Evie snuffled.

We unhugged at the same time, standing up slowly, the cold seeping through my arse. "I should probably go and find Lottie. I didn't mean to yell at her. It's just, sometimes she's really easy to yell at."

Evie shivered but nodded. "I'll come with you. I'm worried about her, Amber. I don't think everything is right with her."

I wrinkled my nose. "You mean a pigeon pooed on her once in wonderful London?"

She shook her head. "Think about it. What does she actually tell us?"

I did what Evie said and thought about it. "Not much," I admitted.

"Exactly. And when does Lottie ever not share? Usually she's all about the sharing. Usually we can't get her to shut up. Haven't you found it weird that she never really says much about uni?"

"Well, no. And now I feel bad."

"Let's go and find her. Maybe she's with Will?"

Lottie was in the front garden, and she wasn't with Will.

She was sitting, her legs sprawled out in front of her, on the lawn. Sobbing.

And, just like that, all my anger fell away. We ran over, slipping in the muddy grass to get to her.

"Oh my God, what happened? Are you okay?" I bent down to touch her bare shoulders. "Lottie, you're freezing. We need to get you inside."

Her entire body heaved with her sobs. "Will..." she said. "Will just broke up with me."

"WHAT?! How?" Evie crouched down too and

rubbed Lottie's arms to try and keep her warm. "We only saw you a few minutes ago."

"It was the countdown to midnight!" I pointed out. "He can't have broken up with you on the countdown to midnight."

Lottie nodded, the motion releasing more tears and snot. "He can and he did."

Evie and I looked at each other. Neither of us were the biggest fans of Will. Ever since we'd got to know him, doing Lottie's Vagilante project last year, he'd been arrogant and superior. Which is sort of why he and Lottie suited each other. But I'd never trusted him – he always overthought things, overcomplicated things. Whenever we hung out, I always felt like he was imagining himself being filmed, like we were all in a movie, and he wanted to be the most articulate character. He never felt that…real.

"What? Why? He's crazy about you," Evie said, rubbing her back more.

Lottie spluttered and gasped to reply. "He said we're too young. That we need to be free."

Evie and I pulled another face at each other. I mean, neither of our boyfriends were saying that. Mine was about to have me come and live in his country, for God's sake.

"What a twat," I said.

"Don't," Lottie heaved. "I'm not ready to hear you call him a twat yet. An hour ago, he was my first proper boyfriend."

"He was still a twat an hour ago," Evie said. "Lottie, Will's always been a bit of a twat."

Lottie lifted her head and her face was a mess, all her eyeliner bleeding out of the black splodges of her eyes. "Will would argue against us using the word 'twat'. He would say we shouldn't base insults on genitalia if we want to be proper feminists."

"See," Evie said, smiling. "Total and utter twat."

Even Lottie laughed, before she started to cry again. And I knew she loved Will, but this crying seemed deeper than that. Harder than heartbreak crying. It was too hollow, too empty, too lonely, even with both our arms around her.

"Lottie, we need to get you inside."

She shook her head. "Can we…go to our bench?" she asked, in a tiny voice.

Our bench…? We hadn't been there in forever. It was on the top of Dovelands Hill, where we all first properly became friends.

"Of course," Evie replied. "Though it's freezing. Can we get our coats first?"

"Let's get more than coats," I said. "Let's really wrap up."

Lottie's cries died down and she gave me a small smile. We still hadn't talked about our fight, or me going to America yet… "Do you not mind leaving the party?"

I smiled back. "Kyle will take care of things. Anyway, it's where we started, isn't it? Sitting on a freezing cold bench after a house party gone wrong?"

We all smiled, until Evie said, "And, if you're leaving, I guess it's where it will all end too."

lottie

I felt numb in all the ways it's possible to feel numb – mentally, literally. My fingers didn't feel like they belonged to my body, neither did my feet…or my heart.

I couldn't believe Will and I were over.

And he'd just walked off, not giving me a chance to argue him out of it. I definitely would've argued him out of it. I'm better at arguing than him.

I had nothing now. No boyfriend, no real uni friends, and I was haemorrhaging old friends too.

"This puffa coat is so puffary I can't put my arms down by my sides," Evie complained, as we walked away from Amber's house, the music getting dimmer as we left it behind us.

Amber and I both looked over and cracked up laughing. "You look like a glow-worm," Amber said.

"No, you look like a foreskin," I added and they both went "EWW, LOTTIE!" and I felt like myself for two whole seconds before jumping back into the abyss of despair again. We'd bundled into every available coat in Amber's cupboard under the stairs, and together sported a weird array of mackintoshes, puffa jackets, and a big piece of fur of Penny's. It was just enough to keep warm. We came across several merrymakers, who all cheered "*Happy New Year*" as we passed. Evie and Amber managed to say it back, whereas I just sniffed and mumbled, "I don't know what's happy about it."

I felt so lost. So thrown away. So…I dunno. Crap? Although that doesn't sound poetic enough. I was still in disbelief about Will, but the Amber news was catching up on me fast, and that was even worse. And all the things she'd said to me tonight. Did she really think I was swanning around in London? Thinking I was too great to spend time with them? I was *drowning* in London. And that was the worst thing. I hadn't realized I could drown and I didn't want to admit it, but I was.

We huffed up Dovelands Hill in awkward silence, none of us quite knowing how to be with each other. And that was what made me really sad. We didn't know how to be around each other any more. Us. The Spinster Club. These girls who I was more honest with than I was with myself. *Was*... The world had rotated only a quarter of the way around the sun, we'd spun on its axis only a hundred times or so, and yet there was a galaxy between us. We were changing, we were growing. Were we growing apart?

The three of us sat on our bench with a thump.

We were. We *were* growing apart. It struck me like I'd been pronged with a giant fork – which I guess I had, in the shed – and I put my head down onto my knees to cry.

"Oh, Lottie, don't cry." Evie reached out from the

many layers of her ridiculous puffa and patted me. "Not over stupid Will."

"I'm not crying about him right now. I'm crying about us."

"Us?" they both echoed.

"Yes. Because it's not the same, is it?" I said, choking on the words, on what they meant. "And we keep pretending it is, but it's really not. And it's going to be even more not when Amber flies away."

I couldn't say any more, I was crying too hard. Not even able to look up at the beautiful view. When no one answered but for snotty sniffles, I realized I'd made the other two cry as well.

"Sorry," I croaked out. "I've ruined your New Year's Eve."

"You've not." Amber reached out and took my frozen hand. She took Evie's too. "And you're right. What the hell is going on with us? I'm sorry I yelled at you, Lotts…"

"I started it. I always start it. No wonder Will dumped me. I'm just a big fat yelling yeller who annoys everyone and everyone just wants to avoid me."

"Woah," Evie said. "Where did that come from?"

I buried my face into my hands again, feeling so low, so sad, so bad about myself. Dumped. A new year and I was dumped. But it wasn't even that. Well, it was that, but it was so much more. I was almost too embarrassed to tell them. Too scared that saying it out loud would make it more real, more humiliating, more horrid.

"I'm really unhappy."

I'd said it. It bellyflopped out into the frozen air, landing with a thump on the hard ground. The world didn't end though. "I'm sorry I haven't invited you girls to uni," I added. "But, well, things haven't been great there..." Amber's hand tightened on mine. "My housemates *hate* me. I've made other friends, on my course, and at the WEP and stuff, but, I mean, I have to live with them every day. I have to sleep there every night. And they're always bitching about me and laughing about me and planning nights out without me, even when I'm there, in the kitchen with them."

"Oh, Lottie," Evie said. "That sounds awful."

"It is..." It was. It felt like releasing poison, admitting

how bad it had been. The giggles coming from the living room, the eye rolls when they found me writing my column on my laptop in the sitting room, that night they brought back essentially the whole rugby team at two a.m., blasted loud music, and I could hear them all laughing and stage-whispering, "*Whoops, we might wake up the FEMINAZI!*"

"Can you not ask to change flats?" Amber suggested.

"I guess I could." I had thought about it. "But isn't that just what social rejects do at uni?"

"No," Evie said. "It's what people do who get put with people they don't get on with. It could happen to anyone."

"I don't know..." I let out a huge exhale of breath that floated off, masking the view for a second before it vanished into the night. "London is amazing...don't pull a face, Amber. It is! But it's also really overwhelming and busy and chaotic. And some amazing stuff has happened – getting my column, the WEP are great, I really think I can make my mark there. But...I'm lonely...I miss you girls."

"And we've missed you!" Amber said. "Why didn't you tell us this was all going on?"

I turned to her. "Well, why didn't you tell us about moving to America? Touché," I added to myself, as an afterthought.

"Lottie, you can't say touché about your own comment," Evie said, giggling, before we all descended into a gloomy quiet.

"I'm sorry I didn't tell you about America," Amber said, puncturing it. "I guess I just didn't want to make it real. I really want to go. It makes sense. But...I don't want to lose you girls."

"You'll lose us by not telling us what's going on in your life," I said.

"Touché again." Amber smiled.

I reached upwards, towards the stars, trying to use the stretch to dislodge all my sadness. "I really thought," I said, "that everything would take off when I started uni. I mean, I turned down Cambridge, which was terrifying, I got through the Vagilante thing, I turned Will into a feminist. I really thought it was going to be my happy ending, you know?"

Amber snorted. "This is life, Lottie. There's no such thing as a happy ending. Because there's no such thing as an ending. More days keep coming, some good some bad. You can't just stay limboed in a moment of happiness – that's not realistic."

"Stop being so wise if you're going to piss off to America."

"I'm not going to 'piss off' to America. We can stay in touch loads."

"Oh, because we've done such a good job doing that when I'm only forty minutes away," I pointed out.

"Well that's your fault, for not inviting us."

"Stop being mean to me, I've just been dumped."

Amber elbowed me. "Ahh, come on, like you'd want to marry someone like Will."

She had a point… I loved him…it hurt it was over… But, well, he always took things very seriously – like he could never be silly and in-the-moment. He always frowned when I tried to make him be like that. And, I'll admit it, I'd felt a bit trapped, like he'd said. There'd been this one night when I met this amazing older guy in a club, who knew who freakin' Mary Wollstonecraft was… I'd been so close to kissing him, because knowing who Mary Wollstonecraft is deserves a kiss at the very least…we were totally into each other…but I'd had to stop…because I was in a relationship…

I was not as upset about Will dumping me as I was about Amber going to America. One was a scribble of biro that I could wash off in time. The other was a tattoo of pain.

I wondered how Evie was taking it?

That's when I realized Evie hadn't said anything for quite a while.

We were where it all began.

Same bench. Same view. Same girls.

And yet totally different girls.

Soon Amber wouldn't even be able to sit on this bench any more.

I listened to how she soothed Lottie, how she opened her up. How she forgave her even though they'd yelled horrid things to each other.

BAD THOUGHT

What if Lottie doesn't want to hang out with you without Amber?

I scratched at my hands, staring out at the sea of yellow lights.

BAD THOUGHT

Everything is falling apart.

But, as I listened to the girls, I realized something. They were right. Things were falling apart because we'd been *keeping things from each other.* Because we'd been trying to face up to things alone rather than facing them together. That's why the threads were breaking. We'd gone off and started new lives and we were too scared to say, not only to ourselves, but to each other, that these new lives weren't going to plan.

"Evie? Evie?" Lottie repeated.

"Huh?"

"You've been very quiet over there, dressed like a foreskin. Is everything okay?"

I knew then that I could nod and pretend and widen the gap. Or I could shake my head and admit that no, I really wasn't all right… But maybe, just maybe, this way I'd get to keep them.

I shook my head, a tear leaking out.

"Oh no." Amber pulled me closer. "What is it?"

"Well, as we're on the subject of not sharing with each other. I've…I've…" I stammered.

BAD THOUGHT

Don't tell them. What if they tell you to break up with him? What if they don't understand?

Good thought

Evie, come on. When have they ever not understood?

"It's Oli," I blurted out. "He's relapsed. Badly. And I don't know what to do."

As the air got colder, I coloured it in for them. How quickly it had come on. How suffocated I felt. How guilty I felt about feeling suffocated. How I was scared his relapse would trigger another one in me. I told them about my night. About his endless messages. His endless need for reassurance. Then I told them about calling him…

There was a silence as the other two digested it all.

"Okay," Amber said slowly. "So tonight is basically a who's-been-keeping-the-biggest-secret competition."

Lottie put her hand up. "Do I win? You know I love winning."

We all sniggered, but our sadness stopped its evolution into laughter.

"Evie, that sounds so tough," Lottie said. "I mean, again, it's not the happily ever after I bet you two painted for yourselves…"

I nodded, clenching my fists, her words sinking in, knowing they were right. This *wasn't* what was supposed to happen. We'd both worked so hard to get better. Us, our love, was our reward. We were supposed to be basking in the harvest of our efforts, not tumbling back down into dark rabbit holes.

"You still love him though?" Amber asked. "You still want to be with him?"

I bit my lip, nodded.

BAD THOUGHT

This is it. This is when they tell you to end it,
this is when you may lose them.

I couldn't breathe.

"Then you'll find a way, Evie," Amber said, and I exhaled so much in relief that I almost passed out. "If you want to make it work, you'll find a way of making it work. It's new though, and it's unfair. You're probably still in the *why-the-hell-has-this-happened-to-me?* period. But once you've grieved that it happened, you can work on boundaries and how to handle your own mental health as well as his."

"Did you just say the words 'grieved that it happened'?" Lottie interrupted. "Holy mother of bumholes, you are American already." Amber whacked her. "Seriously though," Lottie continued. "Amber's right. I think that's what I've been doing too. Mourning the fact my life isn't turning out exactly how it should, especially considering what a brilliant and amazing person I am."

We both thumped her.

"Okay, REALLY seriously now," she laughed.

The grief had melted off her face. Her cheeks were red, her eyes bright. I knew she would hurt about Will, but now I felt it wouldn't be for long. Us not being us had cut off all of our oxygen. We'd all been suffocating. But I didn't think we would let that happen again.

"It sounds hard, but it also sounds like Oli was pretty awesome tonight, when it was you needing him, not him needing you."

"He was. He was amazing." The way he'd taken charge, the way he'd snapped straight into caregiver rather than care-receiver. How he'd got my breathing down, understood exactly what I needed to hear and said it.

"I mean, Will was always terrible when I was upset." Her voice quivered on the word "Will". "He'd always try and logic me out of it, you know? 'That's not reasonable, Lottie. Your housemates aren't that bad, Lottie.' If I was upset and I turned to him, I'd almost always end up feeling worse. But Oli was great to you – because he's been there, because he gets it. And have you thought, maybe, yes, there's a reason for that and there's a downside to that reason, but also it's pretty damn special?"

I started crying. "You've made me cry again."

She was crying too. "I've made me cry again."

"Hey," Amber complained. "I feel left out. Say something deep and meaningful to me so I can cry too."

"You're moving to America?" I suggested.

And, instead of laughing, Amber burst into tears.

We sat and cried, clutching each other for warmth, for stability. It was so cold the tears almost stuck to my cheeks, turning into tiny blobs of ice.

"Look." Amber pointed. "Fireworks."

Off in the distance, the sky turned to glitter and we had our own panoramic view. We lay on the ground, our heads together, and watched the new black sky of this New Year dance and spiral with light. It would be another whole year until the earth was in this exact spot. Another year of growing, changing, learning and, inevitably, being let down by life and the fact that it just keeps going, rather than pausing on the days when everything is going well.

I thought of the three girls who'd sat here over two years ago, on the cusp of a friendship that would change their lives. I thought of what we'd been through since then, the stories we'd made, the people we'd met, how much we'd learned – and yet, tonight we'd learned even more.

We will not let go of the threads of each other. We will not shut each other out.

Life would keep moving on. Things were going to change and evolve. And I was okay with that, as long as we put the work in to make sure our friendship changed and evolved with it.

"What year is it anyway?" Amber asked. "Monkey? Tiger?"

"I think that's Chinese New Year," I said.

"Well, that's just being difficult."

We giggled, until Lottie said, "My arse is SO COLD, can we please go back to the house party where I got horribly dumped so I can exorcize the spirit of it?"

"Yep."

We stood, shaking our limbs, trying to get warmth back into them.

Halfway down the hill, I stopped.

"It's the Year of the Spinster," I said, proudly.

We all paused and looked at each other. The faces I knew so well – that would age and wrinkle, with haircuts that would come and go, and lines that would deepen. Some from laughter, some from sadness. Time would march determinedly on, and we would hold onto each other determinedly as it did so.

"Oh, Eves." Lottie pulled us both in for a hug. "Let's make sure every year is the Year of the Spinster."

THE END

HOLLY BOURNE
on writing, feminism and new year's shenanigans

Having written a book for each of the Spinster Club girls and now the novella too, how do you feel they have grown as characters? Did they develop in the way you originally expected them to?

I'm just so proud of them!! I know they're not real, but they are to me. And seeing them grow from anxious teens attending bad gigs because they feel they should, into mature young women who aren't afraid to call bullshit…it melts my heart. I don't plan my books (which scares my agent – sorry, Maddy!) but I do always have a vague idea of where I want things to go. Before the Spinster Club trilogy this worked fine. But because Evie and Amber and Lottie were so sparky and independent, all three books deviated madly from my outlines. I've been riding their rollercoaster for three years, and it's been the best fun ever (though, yes, admittedly terrifying).

How does your own feminist journey compare to Evie, Amber and Lottie's?

I definitely found it later on in life. I don't think I really considered myself a feminist, or even knew about feminism, until I was about twenty-five. But the day I did, so much fell into place. I finally had a word to describe all the ick I was feeling, and found other people who believed in my ick. Overnight I felt instantly stronger. That's why I wrote these books – to try and get people onto their own feminist journeys as early as possible. Because the quicker we all get there, the quicker we can change the world. I'm jealous that I didn't have Evie, Amber and Lottie at my school. But they're here for my readers, and I hope feminism gives my readers the fire and fun in their lives that it has for me.

Why was it important to you to write about these girls tackling feminist issues?

I think a lot of young people right now feel helpless – like they're too young to change things, too young to be taken seriously, too young to be listened to. I wanted my books to show that this is NONSENSE. That young people can fight, do fight, and can be a giant force to be reckoned with. You are the future, and, by God, from those of you I've met already, this is some kick-ass future. And it's never too early to start reclaiming your future.

**How difficult did you find it switching between three different voices?
And which of the girls do you relate to the most?**

I always found the start of each book tricky, as I'd be mourning being in the previous character's head. I WANT EVIE BACK or I WANT AMBER BACK. I'd have to be really tough in the editing process to make sure Evie's innocence wasn't clambering into Amber's sarcasm, or Lottie's voice wasn't bamboozling its way into...well...everything, as that girl does dominate. I definitely relate the most to Evie, as *Am I Normal Yet?* is the most autobiographical book I'll ever write. But I am cynical and sarcastic like Amber, and, on my good days, I like to think I'm as brave as Lottie.

What have been your own best and worst New Year's Eve experiences?

I honestly cannot think of one New Year's Eve where I've actually enjoyed myself. I hate it. I remember once my friend Rachel got tonsillitis and couldn't come out and I've never been so jealous in my whole life.

So, my worst? Actually, Lottie and Will's demise was inspired by my worst ever New Year – when a guy I'd been seeing on and off decided the countdown to midnight was a good time to tell me it was off for good. Yep. That happened. I left the party at about 12.02 a.m., blubbing my eyes out. But what's so great about being an author is that pain is never wasted! Eleven years later, it's a scene in a book :)

For people like Amber who think that "Nice things don't happen on New Year's Eve" what's the best way to see in midnight without throwing a party?

You need only three things. One, a spoon. Two, a baked Camembert. Three, elasticated trousers.

And finally, what would you say to Evie, Amber and Lottie if they were standing in front of you now?

Umm, dudes? Can I be in your Spinster Club?

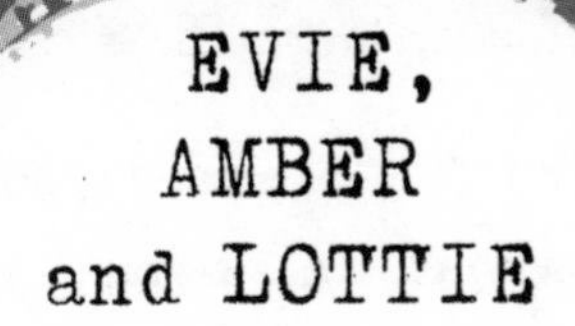

EVIE,
AMBER
and LOTTIE

three girls facing
down tough issues
with the powers of
friendship, feminism
and cheesy snacks

read on to celebrate
the "best bits" of the
SPINSTER CLUB...

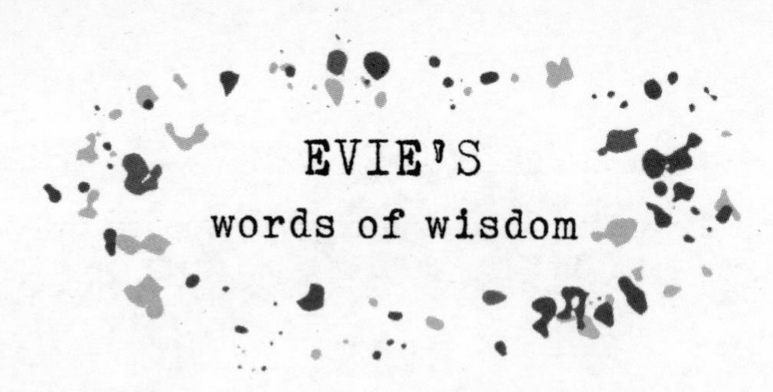

"Mental illnesses grab you by the leg, screaming, and chow you down whole." Am I Normal Yet? chapter 9

"KOOKY!? I'd finally made it down the weirdness spectrum to merely kooky!"

Am I Normal Yet? chapter 2

"'Boink' is retro. It's funnier than 'shag', less cringe than 'make love', and less offensive than 'fuck'."

Am I Normal Yet? chapter 4

"It was all very well being a strong independent woman, but it was hard when boys' confusing behaviour kept making you lose your focus."

Am I Normal Yet? chapter 23

"Just be yourself. Just be happy being you. The best

way to fight girls like Melody is to not buy into all their crap. Be strong, be outspoken, be respected for the right stuff." How Hard Can Love Be? chapter 13

"Was it mental to want someone to love you? Was it mental to want to be courted before you let a guy put an actual piece of his body inside your body? Was it mental to want a message after you'd kissed someone? Was it mental to want the most normal thing in the world – a relationship? One that didn't make your heart feel like it was full of bogeys? Was it mental to not want your heart stamped on until it shattered?"

Am I Normal Yet? chapter 41

"Maybe all the things we fight against – people like you, me, and FemSoc and all the FemSocs around the country – maybe we won't see the change straight away, or at all? But we will have left ripples and some people somewhere in the future will be glad for our ripples and inspired to make their own."

What's A Girl Gotta Do? chapter 23

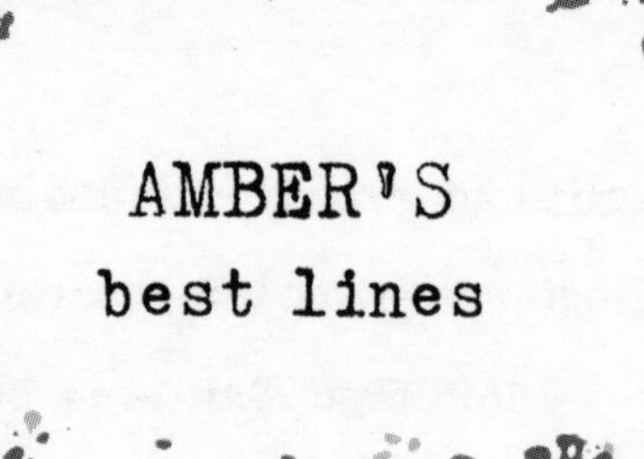

AMBER'S best lines

"Do you ever worry you're being a teenager wrong?"

Am I Normal Yet? chapter 10

"No amount of lovely, romantic hair-tucking will overcome my hair's need to respond to a humid environment." How Hard Can Love Be? chapter 20

"… Shall we save some time here? English people call yards, gardens. And we call jelly, jam. And we call potato chips, crisps. And we call french fries, chips, and… and… And, well, Americans use 'fanny' to describe your butt, and we use the word 'fanny' to talk about OUR BIG ENGLISH VAGINAS, OKAY?"

How Hard Can Love Be? chapter 5

"He made my loins go fluttery."

Am I Normal Yet? chapter 11

"British?" I tried to explain. "We make jokes about uncomfortable topics to feel less awkward about them?"

How Hard Can Love Be? chapter 22

"Sometimes the best things about people are the things that hurt them. Take my feminism for instance – sometimes I think it's not worth it. I get so angry at how unfair it all is and how hard it is to change things. I don't know how…happy it makes me, but it's one of my favourite things about me."

How Hard Can Love Be? chapter 27

"There was the love in life you couldn't choose. The love you just felt, that you couldn't let go of, that tortured you and messed you up and made you sometimes too screwed up to let the other kind of love in. The other kind of love was the love you did choose. The love you didn't have to give, but you gave anyway. Since I'd met Evie and Lottie, I'd begun to learn I was capable of that love."

How Hard Can Love Be? chapter 28

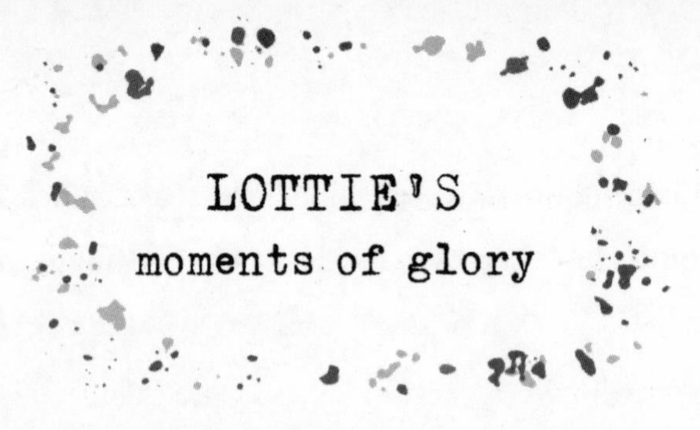

LOTTIE'S
moments of glory

"We can reinvent the word 'spinster', make it the complete opposite of what it means. Like 'young' and 'independent' and 'strong'."

Am I Normal Yet? chapter 20

"Hang on, I need cheesy snacks. I cannot lecture on women's equality without a stash of cheesy snacks…"

How Hard Can Love Be? chapter 13

"The word feminism acknowledges that, since the dawn of time, society historically split humans into two categories – male and female – and one has uncontrollably shat on the other…"

What's A Girl Gotta Do? chapter 11

"I want to be a strong, independent woman with a good career and I don't want my happiness to depend on some bloke on a pony rescuing me."

What's A Girl Gotta Do? chapter 18

"Oh, be still my beating loins."

How Hard Can Love Be? chapter 13

"Maybe all you needed in life was the belief you could change things. Somehow. Some way."

What's A Girl Gotta Do? chapter 9

"Fighting for something you believe in isn't easy. If you hit a sore spot, people are going to swipe at you, gripe at you, try to undermine you, infuriate you, try to shut you up and put you back in your box. I was starting to learn that was a sign you were asking the right questions, picking the right scabs. And though it's easy to lose yourself along the way, and start focusing on all the people who don't want things to change – for whatever broken, messed-up reasons of their own – you can easily find your way back. By listening to the people giving you a hand up. To the people who have your back. To the people who don't think you're a raving lunatic. Let them be your mirror – not the haters. Let them give you the strength to get the job done."

What's A Girl Gotta Do? chapter 46

we asked, you answered.
so here are...
YOUR favourite
SPINSTER CLUB moments

The night the girls first met at the party.
The scene where they go up the hill and sit on a bench after is just <3

Rachel @_sectumsemprah

When Evie destroys stereotypes of mental health in *AINY?* – how ridiculous it is when people say "oh I'm so OCD" etc.

Denise @TheBibliolater

When the girls were having a "vagina meeting" via Skype in *HHCLB?* and Russ and Kyle walked in.

Gem @mountainofbooks

I still love "sexy ferret".

CM Murphy @Cyn_Murphy

I love all the passion for cheesy snacks! And in *How Hard Can Love Be?* I love the girls' Skype calls. And the canoe bit in *How Hard Can Love Be?* And the horn in *What's a Girl Gotta Do?* And…

Alexia Casale @AlexiaCasale

I love Amber's dysfunctional relationship with her mum.

Annalise @AnnaliseBooks

The Sorting in *How Hard Can Love Be?* Amazing way of showing tensions in Amber and her mum's relationship.

Maia @andalittlemoore

Definitely the discussion about periods in *AINY?*

Emily @UncoverAllure

"I know the theme of tonight's meeting is periods but did you really have to get themed biscuits?" Still hilarious.

Something Like Lydia @thinglikelydia

When they remind the boys that their mums have periods.

fictional_and_fabulous via Instagram

When they talk about the Bechdel test because I had never heard of it and couldn't believe how many films don't meet the criteria to pass it!

jcwreads via Instagram

Bechdel test for sure.

hol2205 via Instagram

When Lottie watches the news in *WAGGD?* and realizes how much she talked about a certain someone…

Amber @MileLongBookS

Definitely the moments of Lottie wisdom! Especially when talking about Margaret Thatcher and feminism or lack of. So insightful and just great.

josiecoz via Instagram

I love the scene in *WAGGD?* when Lottie's at her lowest, and the Spinster Club rallies round to read her all the incredible messages of support. Goosebumps!

Rebecca Hill @rebeccashill

The Girl-Next-Door-Slut scene in *AINY?* :)

@holly_bourneYA

see how the spinster club began in:

ISBN: 9781409590309
EPUB: 9781409591467 / KINDLE: 9781409591474

Normal at 16 =

- [x] College
- [x] Friends who won't dump you
- [x] Parties? Fun?
- [ ] A boyfriend?

All Evie wants is to be normal. And now that she's almost off her meds and at a new college where no one knows her as the girl-who-went-nuts, there's only one thing left to tick off her list…

But relationships can mess with anyone's head – something Evie's new friends Amber and Lottie know only too well. The trouble is, if Evie won't tell them her secrets, how can they stop her making a huge mistake?

"Finally, an author who GETS it."
Emma Blackery, YouTuber

follow amber to america in:

ISBN: 9781409591221
EPUB: 9781474915588 / KINDLE: 9781474915595

So I'm spending the summer in CALIFORNIA, with the mum who upped and ABANDONED me – and I think I'm falling for a guy guaranteed to BREAK MY HEART. This is a SITUATION DESTINED TO FAIL.

All Amber wants is a little bit of love. Her mum has never been the caring type, even before she moved to America. But Amber's hoping that spending the summer with her can change all that.

And then there's Prom King Kyle, the serial heartbreaker. Can Amber really be falling for him? Even with best friends Evie and Lottie's advice, there's no escaping the fact: love is hard.

"Holly is the pure, real, honest voice of YA."
Never Judge a Book by its Cover

and see lottie take on
the world in:

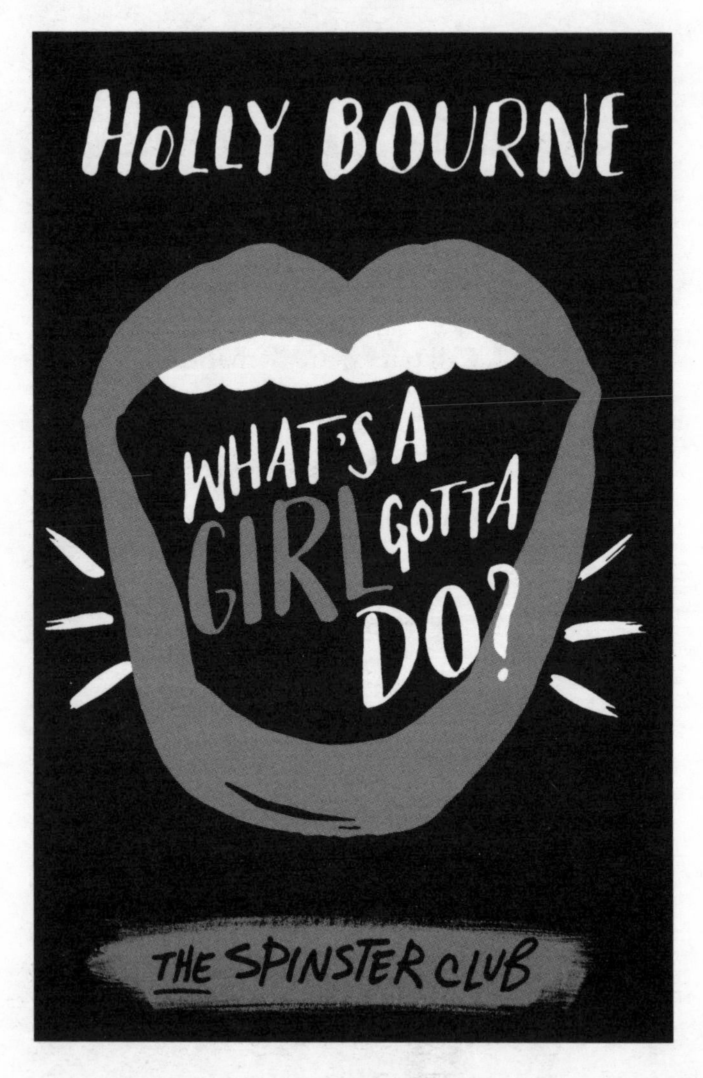

ISBN: 9781474915021
EPUB: 9781474919364 / KINDLE: 9781474919371

HOW TO START A FEMINIST REVOLUTION

1. Call out anything that is
unfair on one gender
2. Don't call out the same thing twice
(so you can sleep and breathe)
3. Always try to keep it funny
4. Don't let ANYTHING slide.
Even when you start to break…

Lottie's determined to change the world with her #Vagilante vlog. Shame the trolls have other ideas…

"A book to press into the hands of every teenage girl you know."
The Bookseller

A LOVE STORY
EIGHTEEN YEARS IN THE MAKING

"A tantalizing story of summer, secrets and deep unease"
MY SECRET LIES WITH YOU
FAYE BIRD

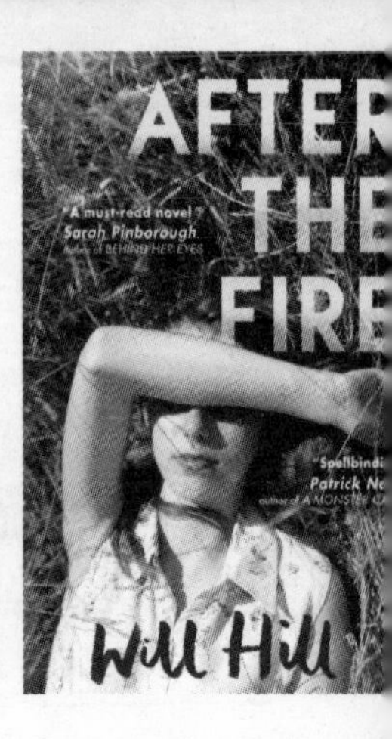
AFTER
"A must-read novel"
Sarah Pinborough
Will Hill

USBORNE
YA

@UsborneYA

"A pure joy from start to finish"
Brian Conaghan Costa-winning author
ROSIE LOVES JACK
Mel Darbon

"Magical...really captures the feeling of being in love."
CASSANDRA CLARE, author of THE MORTAL INSTRUMENTS series
ANNA and the FRENCH KISS
AN INTERNATIONAL BESTSELLER
STEPHANIE PERKINS

The Last